EDGE OF THE LAND

EDGE OF THE LAND

BOOK 3

THE MERSEYSIDE CRIME SERIES

MALCOLM HOLLINGDRAKE

This edition produced in Great Britain in 2024

by Hobeck Books Limited, 24 Brookside Business Park, Stone, Staffordshire ST15 0RZ

www.hobeck.net

A CIP catalogue for this book is available from the British Library.

ISBN 978-1-915-817-41-9 (pbk)

ISBN 978-1-915-817-40-2 (ebook)

Cover design by Jayne Mapp Design

Front cover image © Ian Cleverdon

Printed and bound in Great Britain

Dedicated to
Danny Norkus

A dear friend and colleague.

No man is free who cannot control himself

Pythagoras

CHAPTER 1

The cold of the early morning penetrated her gloves bringing a sting to her fingers. The gusting wind slapped her face as it channelled its way down the narrow valley that was home to the Leeds and Liverpool Canal as well as that of the railway linking Wigan to Southport. The isolated area at this time of day seemed to belong only to nature. The cold contradicted the warmth generated from the expelled energy, as sweat clung to Skeeter's lower back where it dribbled and pooled. Her breath, steady and rhythmic, immediately emitted small clouds of grey vapour in regular streams, as warm gasps were forced from her gaping mouth.

The canal seemed to be breathing, too, as smoky wisps clung in a filigreed mantel along its dark surface, the dawn light bringing with it a silver, ghost-like curiosity. Pausing momentarily, she stood by what once was the lock keeper's cottage and enjoyed the low sun's first warmth. It made her face tingle. The viaduct carrying the M6 crossed the valley at this point, overshadowing the railway and the canal. The history of transport was captured all within a few metres. She knew this moment of contemplation to be a distraction, it always was. She was deflecting the one thought that came to mind at this point of the run – the hill, her everyday nemesis that stood a mile away between here and home – Bank Brow. The long climb snaked from Appley Bridge up towards Roby Mill and her cottage. It had the potential to become the final straw as the incline increased and the burn grew within leg muscles and lungs. The less strong might just relax their pace and walk the last few hundred yards as the incline increased. Skeeter Warlock was determined, driven as she spat on the road, a signal demonstrating her pure disdain at the very thought of surrender. She had adopted her mantra, *By any available means or method*, the code by which she had lived her life since her teens, a time she preferred to leave in the dark. It had been carefully tattooed in Latin on what was normally a concealed area of her body; the script was delicate and subtle. It was always there, as an aide-mémoire should she find herself with her back to the wall. Her right hand moved, and her fingers caressed the area, as if reading by braille, that small act filling her with a renewed energy.

Skeeter stood at the gate to her cottage, her hands resting on her thighs as she fought to control her breathing. She was filled with a mixture of exhilaration and endorphins, nature's home brewed opiates. It brought a smile. The path from the road to the front door was bordered by a hedge. She checked her watch. It was just after 6.15. Rising onto her tiptoes, she looked over the privets at her neighbour's path. Tom was usually on his second cigarette and pacing up to the gate and back, but today, the strong smell of tobacco was absent. It was a smell that took her back to school and the old steel container where redundant furniture was stored. His absence was unusual but then, considering his age, a warm bed might just have been too inviting.

* * *

The lead held in the owner's hand seemed to stretch for ever as the dog sniffed the rough, grassed areas to the side of the footpath. She seemed oblivious, transfixed to her phone screen, trying to respond to a number of messages with both hands occupied. Although the early morning was cold, the surrounding trees and the park's location offered a degree of protection from any coastal breeze. She had walked some distance within Hesketh Park, a route she travelled daily during the working week.

The brick building that housed the old astronomical observatory sat at the upper end of the footpath. It was as if the dog were divining as it swung on a horizontal, flexible pendulum until, in the fullness of time, it had eventually completed three hundred and sixty degrees before the lead wrapped her legs.

'Casper!' The frustration was clear in her voice as she was momentarily distracted from responding on her phone. She stepped out of the looped lead as she reeled in the dog.

'Behave, Casper!' She neither looked at the dog nor her surroundings, as her phone instinctively came back to her face. The dog also paid little attention as it tried to move off again. Casper barked, tugging at the lead until her finger released the lock. The dog ran in the direction of the observatory and the bench positioned close by, extending the umbilical cord that prevented total freedom to the maximum. Without Casper's incessant barking she would not have taken notice of the bench, nor the person seated. The morning walk was a vital time for her to catch up on emails as well as exercise the dog before leaving for work. Her routine brought with it a complacency, as if she seemed to know every blade of grass, whether it be in the clock garden, or near the fountain, and so the dome topped building was invisible: there, but unseen. Even the people she met always seemed to be at the same places at the same times! Yet today, even though everything seemed normal, that familiarity would change, and Hesketh Park would never be the same place again.

CHAPTER 2

April Decent drove down Leeward Drive, Speke, before turning into the Operational Command Centre of Merseyside Police. She parked her 4x4 as directed after speaking to the security office. The relatively new flagship station was built on the site of the old Speke Airfield. The freshness and order of the building seemed in total contrast to Copy Lane and the old HQ at Canning Place but matched that of the new HQ at Rose Hill. These buildings defined the financial commitment to policing in Merseyside and they filled her with a degree of pride in the fact she had taken the leap and moved to work there. The Command Centre was planned to house officers dealing with serious and organised crime and putting all under one roof had seemed logical. The sub-divisional stations would still operate but their role would change with time. Policing had been in a state of flux from the very beginning. As crime and criminality changed, so, too, did the response and fight against it.

The formality and, for her, the modern architecture, seemed like a breath of fresh air. The sun still proved reluctant to appear and the morning seemed cold. Tico, her rescue greyhound, had shown similar signs of disdain whilst on their morning walk along the beach and was happy to return to the Aga and the bed set before it. He had allowed the barriers to fall between himself and Sky, the farmer's border collie. They now enjoyed time together. Sue Martin, the owner of April's rented cottage, often took him for the day allowing the dogs to play in the yard and become friends. It had taken some time, but their initial antipathy had waned.

Passing through the glass barrier, she smiled at the security officer and collected her lanyard. They passed the time of day. The first time she had seen the interior of the building it had taken her breath away and each time she entered she would stand momentarily to enjoy the spacious setting.

Skeeter had followed her in.

'Morning.' Skeeter's grin was infectious. 'You'll get used to it when we move here, and it'll just become your place of work – same old!' She winked and twisted around whilst throwing her arms out wide. 'Not too dissimilar to the old place, April. I'll kind of miss the view from my window.'

'What view?'

'*Sod all view*. It had a certain charm. At least I'll be able to bring the leaded window you kindly made for me.'

April's phone rang.

'Boss!' It was Lucy Teraoka. She paused before continuing.

April looked at Skeeter who raised her eyebrows and rubbed her hands. The day had started in earnest.

Lucy finished giving her report.

'We'll be an hour. Are people from Southport on it?'

'Yes, but I've sent Tony, too, as we have another investigation locally.'

* * *

6

DC Tony Price stood with his back to the gates of the wrought iron steps that led to the upper floor of the observatory and chewed the nail of his left thumb. There was little to work on but he was making a gallant effort to get something for his endeavour. Eventually admitting defeat, he wiped his nose on the back of his hand as he stared at the police tape stretched from either side of the steps towards the trees to each side of the bench. Further tape closed the rear of the large triangle. Two PCSOs were positioned on the footpaths that approached the site. Temporary makeshift screens had been erected around the bench and the on-call doctor worked unseen. The notes he had received from the attending officer were tucked in his pocket. No identification could be found on the body, there was neither watch nor wallet. It seemed the man was a vagrant considering the state of his clothing and his lack of cleanliness. That fact alone would make finding the man's identity difficult.

A flatbed golf-type cart, normally used by the park gardening staff, was positioned to one side of the building. Kerry Fisher sat alongside the paramedic, a foil blanket wrapped around her shoulders. Tony waited patiently until he saw the hand signal suggesting she was fit enough to be questioned.

'She's shaken, but that's understandable. She's also on edge about her dog, it's been taken to a vet. However, she wants to talk about it. I'm here if you need me.' The paramedic patted Tony's shoulder.

Tony sat next to her and introduced himself.

'Is he … dead?' Her immediate question was supported in a voice that was more controlled. It surprised him – witnesses tended to be less in control.

'We'll know more once the doctor's checked things out—' He did not finish before she spoke.

'Casper found him, you know that? Wouldn't leave him alone. He jumped on the bench and then the man's knee. I had to take the bottle from Casper. Medicinal, maybe tablets, so my friend's rushed him to the vet. The paramedic advised it.' She turned to look at the man who was in conversation with the doctor by the police tape.

Tony was trying to get things into some chronological perspective. He knew from the first responder that an empty bottle of vodka had been found under the bench and the dog had found a small brown bottle that might have contained drugs of some kind. There was no label attached. It had brought it to its owner and dropped it proudly at her feet. There was no lid; that was still near the bench.

'I thought he was dead as he just seemed to slump slightly to one side when I touched his arm. His face was the strangest colour, as if he'd seen a ghost. Grey, pale. There was no warmth, either. It was then I rang for help.'

'You've done well and we're grateful. There was nothing more you could have done.'

Her mobile rang and she immediately answered.

'How's Casper?' There was anxiety evident in her voice. She looked directly at Tony before lowering her head. 'Thank goodness for that.' A smile broke across her face. 'Thank you. I'll be home soon.'

Tony nodded. 'Sounds as though he's fine.'

'They found nothing in the stomach contents to cause concern. They'll keep him for another few hours as a precaution, but he should be fine.' She breathed deeply. 'What's strange, officer, is that if Casper hadn't been near the man I'd have just walked past. Never given him a second thought.'

'Others might have done that earlier but then it would have been dark. From my experience, you wouldn't have been the first in that respect. People have busy lives and in today's society some are reluctant to interfere. You'd be surprised to learn how many bodies are found by dog walkers or early morning runners. You found him and you did the right thing. There's nothing more you could have done for him. I've arranged for someone to take you home when you feel ready.'

She smiled and began to remove the foil blanket.

'Keep it on until you're home.' He helped draw the foil around her shoulders. 'We may need to chat with you again once we know more.'

The doctor watched as Tony approached him whilst a female PCSO helped the woman down the path to where a car would be waiting by the gate. The doctor removed his face mask, the last item of PPE, and deposited it into a yellow plastic container along with the rest before collecting his bag.

'All the makings of a suicide, Tony. I'd put the time of death between eleven and three this morning, but as you know, that's an approximation owing to the temperature fluctuations we are experiencing at the moment. The bottle the dog retrieved will be analysed, but I feel it contained something that, when taken alongside a large quantity of vodka, had the effect he might well have desired. He came, it's very quiet after dark, sat here at whatever time, consumed goodness knows what along with a bottle of booze, and that was it – Goodnight Vienna! I'll have a greater understanding once we do a post-mortem. It could be lorazepam or diazepam and either of those in quantity washed down with vodka would have the potential to kill. Alcohol after midnight has two to three times more psychomotor effects than when consumed earlier in the day. The drug, if it is what I suggest, even if taken a day or so before, could still create a lethal cocktail. So, it might be accidental, but in my judgement more likely suicide.'

Tony nodded remembering somewhere in the past he had heard that about time and booze.

'Teaching my grandfather to suck eggs, I guess, Tony. Funny, there were no signs of vomit or traces on or near the bench which did surprise me a little if he'd consumed what was in the bottles we saw.'

Tony frowned.

'Is that a common result of the drug or the vodka or both?'

'Even just the vodka, as I guess that wasn't all he'd had last night. His coat had been the recipient in the past, but the staining was not necessarily from the last couple of days. Vagrants have a capacity to consume a good deal when they have the cash.'

* * *

James Speakman stood on the bank of the canal. A sizeable pile of timber lay at his feet. Many were large branches foraged from the nearby woodland. He collected whenever he could, after all, it was free. The canal barge, his home for the last five years, was not the most attractive craft moored just outside Haskayne. The cosmetic appearance was the least of his considerations. He would wash it when it rained, if the mood took him. As often as not, it remained dirty but for the odd painted mural, fancy buckets and what he called *tranklements* – a misuse of the word but now meaning the canal boat art that so often added splashes of colour to the travellers' everyday objects and seen on most canal leisure craft – were not for him. Those present when he purchased the craft were all on display, along with the name emblazoned down the side of the rear of the cabin – *Arcanum*. It was a working boat, his home and his escape, and, like him, it should be plain and simple.

The axe split the wood into manageable lengths before he sectioned some into kindling with a saw. Each pile was to be loaded into different net-like plastic bags. Even the chippings did not go to waste; his collection was meticulous. Once loaded, he leaned on the edge of the boat, lit a roll-up cigarette and stared across at the opposite bank. It seemed overly busy with cyclists and dog walkers, considering the time of day.

Mooring opposite the canal path was always preferable; it ensured solitude and security from the occasional feral youths who could prove troublesome. He had made wooden porthole covers to guard against stone throwers and he always kept a catapult and a collection of steel nuts should he need to repel anyone seeking trouble. It was rarely used but he enjoyed spending the odd half an hour honing his accuracy.

Smoke, grey and fine, drifted from the black chimney stack at the rear of the boat. Breaking the morning's peace, the whistle of a kettle grew more urgent, its shrill alarm call only too clear. He chuckled and flicked the remnants of the cigarette over the boat and into the canal. 'Slowly, slowly wins the race, James.' He moved to the back of the boat whilst blowing on his hands.

* * *

Tony addressed April. 'Looks like suicide. Man in his fifties. From his appearance he's a dropout. No ID but we'll put out photographs on the website, might jog someone's memory. From the people I've seen and interviewed he's not a regular in the park and the local PCSO hadn't seen him around the town.' Tony trapped the phone beneath his chin as he searched his pockets for the car keys.

'I'll inform the coroner and we'll await the autopsy. What time was he found?'

'The call came in at just after six, it was growing light. What's amazed me is the resilience of dogs,' Tony muttered.

'Sorry?' April looked towards the window at the far side of her office, confused by his last statement.

'Casper, the dog who discovered the chap, might well have consumed what was left in the medicine bottle but according to the vet he seemed fine. If he ate what the doc thinks the chap had and remained standing, he would be one resilient hound.'

'Diazepam or some other prescription drug?' April chipped in.

Tony's hands stopped patting his clothing, he had found his keys and was grateful for the warmth of the car.

'His words exactly. How did ...' He let his question drop. 'He mentioned diazepam. I looked it up, Valium.'

April raised her eyebrows surprised at his enthusiasm for the case.

'I believe you're following up on the incident of yesterday evening reported by a Wayne Beales. The location is relatively close.'

She read the address, but she was wrong, it was quite a drive. Tony had been made aware of the call that came in and the need for clarification of the incident.

'Speak with Mr Wayne Beales. There seems some contradiction in the stories. The intruder is known to him and I'm inclined to listen to him rather than the story Danny Maynard told the officers attending last night, but don't let that sway your judgement. I'll see you back here.'

Tony tossed his phone onto the passenger seat and muttered under his breath. 'Joy. Danny Bloody Maynard!' He tapped the address into the satnav.

CHAPTER 3

D anny Maynard was considered nothing more than a misguided youth who had borne the heavy cross of a troubled and cruel upbringing. He was lost to education and had found drugs early, the way to fund his habit being to either steal or trade. When in trouble or needing refuge, he would call on a housebound elderly relative, his maternal uncle, who would either give shelter, cash or both whenever he called. This refuge became more the norm as time passed. By the age of sixteen, it had more or less become his permanent home. Many who lived near saw it as abuse, but the uncle could see no wrong in his nephew. Danny, on the other hand, did not understand the meaning of loyalty and would often trade his wares to school kids on the local estate unaware of the mantra – *you shouldn't shit on your own doorstep* – or, in this case, that of your uncle! His relationship with the police had been mixed, his propensity to drive stolen vehicles without a licence or insurance resulted in a quad bike being removed from his uncle's garage. Feeling that was unacceptable, he had marched down to St Anne Street Police station threatening to burn it down if they refused to return his property. The culmination of his misdemeanours resulted in a prison sentence.

Tony parked and checked the details. The homes were a mix of bungalows and dormers, each with a small front garden. Only a few cars were parked on the road, as many occupants would be at work. It was not to Maynard's uncle's house he had to go, but next door. For a welcome change, he was greeted warmly, shown in and was pleased to be offered a coffee.

'Thanks for coming. It happened just after nine last night. My wife and I had settled down to watch the TV when the front door burst open and Danny came crashing into the lounge with blood pissing from a huge gash on his head. He was like the proverbial bull in a fucking china shop. I have to admit I nearly shit myself, what with him and the wife's screams. To be honest, I was worried who was coming in after him, and with seeing all the blood I wondered what weapons they might have!' Wayne frowned. 'I checked outside but there was no one about.'

Tony looked down and could still see a faint trail of blood staining on the carpet and rug like two, thin dark snail trails.

'We've used the Vax cleaner on it twice, but I don't think it will come out! There's also blood on the chair and the wall there.' He pointed to the various locations as he shook his head. 'Danny told me three people had been waiting. They attacked him when he left next door and hit him hard with something metal. He turned and dashed in here damaging the door in his attempt to get away from them. We rang for the police and an ambulance but were told that the ambulance would take two hours. The police arrived within fifteen minutes, but you'll know that. They offered to take him to A&E but Danny refused.'

'And he told my colleague when questioned that he fell. Is that right?' Tony sipped his coffee.

'He did. I couldn't believe it. He'd only just told me the real story, but I guess with our Danny he wouldn't know the truth if it slapped him in the face. He's always had a creative imagination ever since he was a nipper.'

'Or if reality cracked him on his head?' Tony muttered, frustration clearly showing in his voice.

'I know his past, known him since he was knee high and I know the kind of upbringing he's had so I always try to help him. He pestered the life out of me to mend his knackered bikes or to let him wash my car. Always bloody fiddling. The rest of the road would happily see him hanged! I kept telling him he'd end up a no-mark, a wastrel, a nobody living in doorways and empty buildings. We've enough of those already. I told him he needed to do well at school, get a job, pay taxes and get some self-respect – don't try to be the king of clowns in the circus of clowns you're messing with now. I tried all ways to make him see the errors of his ways, tried to re-educate him. I try with a few people, it's in my nature, I'm told. I'll tell you one thing, you could ask him anything about geography, where places are in the world, and he'd tell you. You know why?' He looked at the officer.

'No idea, Mr Beales,' Tony answered, uncertain as to the relevance and lack of interest.

'When he wouldn't co-operate, when he misbehaved or wouldn't sit still in class, he was made to face the wall, the same wall every time and on that wall was a map of the world. He must have looked at that map for hours on end. I never thought he was thick, just misguided and easily led.' He paused briefly as if to catch his breath. 'If I asked him where in the world was Timbuktu, he'd tell me straight off. Do you know?'

Tony shook his head. He wanted to say on the Wirral but thought better of it.

'Me neither, but he did. As I said, he just seemed to want to be king clown. Here's a thought for what it's worth, maybe his talking with your people, the bizzies, would be classed as *grassing* and that would get him into more bother with the nutters he's tangled up with?'

'The thugs who do this have little sympathy. I suggest if or when he returns here or next door, you call us. Don't try to help him if he's confronted again. If he's pissed off the clown circus, as you call it, they'll seek their money, the drugs he might have stashed, or maybe they're seeking retribution for all three. What I do know from my own limited experience in the job is they'll want their pound of flesh to deter others from doing the same and in time they'll get it, and they'll make it known. Remember, they can be most ruthless.'

'So where does that leave us?' Wayne Beales's eyes showed clear anxiety as he spread his arms.

'Was your door locked?'

Wayne shook his head.

Tony sighed. 'I suggest it should always be locked. We'll add some extra patrols.'

'Extra!' Wayne stood and laughed. 'The only time we see you people is when you're looking for Danny. Other than that, a copper walking in this estate is a thing of the past, they're extinct creatures in the suburbs of Merseyside and you know it.'

Tony drained his coffee cup. 'He's done the time required for the crimes he committed and he's now in temporary accommodation until more permanent housing can be found.' His facial expression suggested he did not agree with either the location or the support. 'It seems from what you've told me he hasn't changed. Trust me, Mr Beales, further enquiries will be made if not for the lad's sake but for people like yourselves, the innocents who get caught in the crossfire. You should not be in this position, particularly when he hides the truth from us.'

* * *

DS Skeeter Warlock was finalising some paperwork. She had secured the arrest of five individuals who had been transporting stolen high-end 4x4s from around the north west. It had been a long and complex case with the need for co-operation with colleagues in Europe. Many of the cars had been destined for Ireland. Working with the Proactive Policing Unit they had managed to break up the group and had made a number of arrests whilst securing the vehicles. She looked up as Tony entered.

'Bit early for night school, Tony.' She made a deliberate attempt to look at her watch.

'Bugger off, Wicca. I was here when you were still in your pit.' He opened his desk drawer and pulled out two cans of Coke. He tossed one towards his colleague. 'Catch! Hopefully, it'll blow your head off when you open it!' He winked. 'Cheers!'

Skeeter Warlock had been initially known as *Witch*, owing to her *heterochromia iridum*. At school it had been a cross Skeeter had to bear and it was there her nickname, Witch, had stuck, the name she had also carried during her early years in the force. In time, particularly to those close to her professionally and those at the wrestling gym, she was generally known as *Wicca*, the derivative of the word *witch*. It seemed apposite, but it had been given not because of her unusual stare, but because of her name. It was something she embraced.

'Attended a suicide this morning, Hesketh Park of all places. Oldish chap. Was sitting there as if he didn't have a care in the world.' He sipped more of his Coke before moving over and perching on the side of Wicca's desk.

'Profound! I'd suggest he was more worried about meeting St Peter and what was in store for him in the next life, Tony.'

'Right, it was just his peaceful appearance. Why are suicides, and bodies for that matter, usually always found by dogs or joggers?' He let the question hang and Skeeter failed to state the obvious. 'Have you ever thought why people do it? Christ, they must be in a position where they can't talk to anyone, the end of the road, the bottom of the lowest pit of emotional trauma.'

Skeeter leaned forward and put both hands in the waste bin as she pulled the tab on the can. There was a fizz and a rush of Coke as it ran down the side of the bin. 'No damage done. Just to show you there are more ways of killing a pig than stuffing it full of cherries, Tony.' She grinned and sipped the Coke before continuing. 'I think drink and tablets is an easy route. I could never understand those who jump off buildings or step in front of trains. A year back, one jumped off the roof of the old Midland railway warehouse, it's now something to do with Liverpool museums, a warehouse for their precious art works. He died but he also seriously injured a pedestrian below. To think you're going about your everyday business and your life ends or changes dramatically in a minute, all because someone has lost the will to survive.' She shook her head. 'If you're determined to do it follow your chap's example.'

Tony looked down at her wanting to change the subject whilst thinking about Wayne Beales and his wife. 'Danny Maynard!'

Skeeter looked up and leaned back in her chair. It seemed to be a non sequitur but her interest was sparked. 'Tell me more. Tell me more!' She sang.

'That was Danny Zuko!' He raised his eyebrows. 'Keep up as we ask bloody questions at the end! No, my Danny is our regular no-mark kid who's no longer a kid, who just can't get straight and doesn't want to accept any kind of responsibility. He's not long been released and he's still supported by our taxes; he's in paid accommodation.'

'It was ever thus. Go on.'

'He burst into a neighbour's house last night seeking protection, or to escape from what I assume to be people he's truly pissed off. His unorthodox entry scared the crap out of the couple who'd been kind to him since he was very young. Danny told the police attending that the reason for a massive head wound was on account of a fall; a fucking fall, can you believe, what with whatever brains he had hanging from his hair? The daft bugger had even told Beales the real story. These people are the liabilities, Wicca, just like your diver off the roof. They should just be locked away.'

'What did Beales say?'

'He remained schtum but his face told a very different story. If I'm honest, there was real concern. I spoke with the officer attending but his hands were tied. If the guy won't co-operate, there's little they can do. The fear of being labelled *a grass* can be truly intimidating, as you well know.'

'Let's hope he has more than one guardian angel as there are enough devils out on these streets.' Skeeter tossed the empty Coke can into the bin.

'By the way, where's Timbuktu?'

'Mali and that's in West Africa when I last looked but I don't check too often.'

Tony frowned. 'Not the Wirral, then?'

Skeeter laughed.

* * *

Danny Maynard pulled the woollen beanie hat cautiously down toward his eyebrows and felt the pain from the jagged gash that ran for an inch and a half just above his left ear. It had bled intermittently throughout the night creating an ugly pattern on the pillowcase. If he had had a needle and some fishing line, he would have attempted to stitch it himself but just running his finger around the wound made him wince. His imaginary bravery had never matched reality; he had experienced that misguided belief throughout his short life. He knew who had attacked him and he knew the reason. He looked in the mirror. 'The best form of defence is to attack, right?' His words were uttered with neither conviction nor confidence, and as he spoke, he felt the fear grow in the pit of his stomach and rise to his throat making him vomit.

The accommodation was rudimentary at best but it was warm. Being handed your own toilet roll on arrival set the standard and the condition of the shared toilets varied, their cleanliness was usually determined by those using them, and from what he had experienced so far, they demonstrated few rules of general hygiene. Other residents, coming from different backgrounds, seemed to keep themselves to themselves or found soul mates depending on the length of time they were there. Often, they were the people you could trust, but Danny had found no one he liked.

He needed fresh air, a walk, but a walk on busy streets. He knew the last thing he needed right now was to go back to his old haunts. His uncle had slipped him some cash and that should last him a few days.

From York Street he moved towards the river. The gulls' calls, carried on a cutting wind, seemed to scream louder than he remembered the closer to the water he walked. The Albert Dock was always busy, a place to meld amongst the many strangers. Since his release, time seemed to hang. He knew he could never repay the money he owed when arrested, but nor would he, not without work or a lucky lottery ticket. The consequences of that knowledge throbbed in his head. He had asked his uncle but he had nothing. His mother could not and would not help. She had washed her hands of him.

The Albert Dock was always busy with the number of shops and restaurants sited alongside the Tate Gallery and the Maritime Museum. Resting against one of the many red stanchions, he let his gaze take in the central pool of water. A few boats were moored along the edge, they were of little interest; he only glanced at each but his eyes did not linger long. Walking from the dock, he headed towards the Liver building, passing the pier master's house before pausing momentarily at the statue of Billy Fury. He looked at the plaque; at least he had managed to learn to read at school. He had never heard of him.

'Great singer, Billy Fury.' The voice from behind startled him. 'You're too young. Died before you were born.'

Danny felt uncomfortable as the stranger seemed too familiar.

'Are you from Liverpool?' He put the cigarette to his lips and lit it allowing the smoke to drift from his nostrils. 'Sorry, rude of me.' He held the packet towards Danny.

Danny paused; the reluctance was clearly masked on his face. He studied the man's features.

'Take one. I want to ask a favour.'

Danny stepped back.

'Could you take a photograph of me with Billy?' He held the phone out alongside the packet of cigarettes. 'I'm also going to get one with the Beatles later. You heard of the Beatles?'

Danny nodded and lifted his shoulders taking the phone and a cigarette; he popped the cigarette carefully into the brim of his beanie hat before taking the picture. He quickly relaxed. 'I'll take one more to be on the safe side.'

The man changed pose, putting his finger against the extended hand of the statue. Danny handed back the phone.

'Thanks.' He checked the pictures, smiled and turned to cross the bridge. 'Great photographs. Take care and have a good day. Maybe see you around.' Within a minute he was heading towards the Museum of Liverpool.

'Maybe not.' Removing the cigarette, Danny rolled it below his nose and enjoyed the nutty smell. He would have it later.

'Billy Fury,' the words were but a whisper. 'What a bloody great name unlike Daniel Maynard. Maybe if I'd been born a Billy, I might have gone places.' Nodding at the statue he followed the same direction as the stranger towards Mann Island. He paused, just over the bridge that crossed the huge lock gates. Along the chain fence to his right were hundreds of padlocks, differing in size and colour; many appeared to have been there for a long time. Pausing, he noticed some were engraved with names and dates. Some were shiny and new whilst others were rusting from the Mersey's salt laden air.

He heard a couple close by refer to them as 'love locks'. Looking at the number attached there was an awful lot of love. If only he had received his fair share, he might not be in the position he was now.

CHAPTER 4

Peter Firth reversed the white DAF, manoeuvring the tipper trailer through the narrow gap. His head moved to look in the two mirrors, whilst following the instructions that came from the waving hands until he saw them cross. He was in position. The cover of the trailer was wound back, exposing the contents before the container began to rise. Peter put his hands behind his head and stretched. It had been a long day. Climbing from the cab he walked to the rear of the wagon to check the load had been discharged. It had. Moving back to the cab he lowered the tipping body, gave the thumbs up and drove the wagon out onto the dock road.

Danny pulled the collar of his coat up against the breeze that seemed to funnel down the river to find every gap and crevice between the buildings. The lights had already started to appear – myriad colours against the growing grey of the evening. He sat, hands round a large cup of coffee and stared at the Ferris wheel in the distance and the reflections in the round pond and water fountain in the landscaped area near Liverpool One. The cyclopic eye of a CCTV camera directly to his left offered a degree of security. He would head home soon, if that is what the single room could be called. As far as he could see, life at the moment offered little; a claustrophobic feeling of failure began to wrap him in a firm yet invisible grip.

Victoria Griffiths pushed the supermarket trolley along Bankhall Street. Eeyore, the small, bedraggled toy was fastened, like a mascot, to the front by a red plastic tie. It nodded as if in its last throes of life. The rusting basket on wheels was filled with her worldly goods, on which sat a small cardboard box containing the daily food donations generously supplied by the café at the bottom of the road. If she called late there was always something, a coffee and some food, whatever was left. She was as regular as the many paying customers. As a gesture of goodwill she never overstayed her welcome, knowing her appearance and the aroma that followed in her wake, a distinctive smell of loneliness that could linger for some time after she had left, could be a reason for future rebuttal. If anything, she preferred to loiter just away from the door, where she would wave and attract the attention of the staff. She continued as one wheel kicked and flapped sideways having a mind of its own. Occasionally, she would kick it straight. Trapped within the various blankets that lined the base of the trolley basket, was a bottle of vodka along with some cans of strong lager. 'My secret stash,' she called it. It was her recipe to hold back the cold and suspend the memories of times gone by.

The brick warehouse, built in 1874, according to the date set high within both alcoves positioned some distance apart on the building's façade, was semi-derelict. It was empty and had been for as long as she could remember, although the land to the rear was occasionally used to store skips and containers. The blind windows were boarded with steel plates on the lower level, the glass smashed in many of those above. They made sad reminders of the lack of respect for the once thriving grandeur of this and the other structures that once filled the area, where this particular stretch had played a key part in creating and maintaining the city's wealth. Today, the narrow, sprawling mass that bordered the River Mersey still held several miles of docks and warehouses in various stages of life and death. Now, just like Victoria Griffiths, the best was behind them, the land lay raped and torn. For some areas there was a future, but for others, only continued decay. For Victoria, this small part of the city was manageable, almost private and it was home.

She pushed the supermarket trolley into one of the cart-width alcoves that sat well away from the pavement. To the left, someone had fly tipped four tyres. They had not been there earlier in the day when she had ventured into the city. The alcoves had once been the loading bays. She had parked her trolley there each night for as long as she could remember. She removed the bagged contents and dropped them over the low wall, part of the canal bridge positioned at the canal end of the building. Following them over, she slid clumsily across the coping stone whilst holding on to the vodka. The large buddleia sprawled over the top of the wall, a mass of purple flowers, hiding her entry and an aid when climbing back. The narrow grassy bank just below her ran for only a few feet along the canal side before meeting the semi-derelict loading shed. The roof held by metal columns, yet open to the canal side in places, offered a security from rain and wind. In the time she had been coming there she had never been disturbed, only by rats and the other creatures of the night. It was her sanctuary, a place to keep clothes and the paraphernalia collected from bins and charity that she did not need on her daily excursions.

Sniffing the cold sausage sandwiches made her stomach rumble and her mouth water. She never rushed a meal; good, clean food was precious and deserved to be savoured at a leisurely pace, after all, she still had her dignity, which could never be lost nor stolen. As she ate, she drank from one of the cans of lager. Once replete, she lay on an old mattress positioned on wooden pallets. She had covered them with whatever was to hand to lift her from the damp ground and offer a degree of comfort whilst propped against bags of clothing and more stacked pallets.

A satisfying belch echoed within the empty space. She giggled, but within an instant, she stopped as the sudden smell of tobacco, faint yet sweet, drifted momentarily into her nostrils. A silent alarm bell rang in her head as a tingle of fear came to her stomach and she felt the nausea and the acidic taste of food filling her mouth. She lay still allowing her eyes to scan the poorly lit area from right to left. There was no one on the opposite bank of the canal, as far as she could see. She leaned forward to allow her vision to clear the wooden canopy. Someone was there. A vague silhouette could be seen on the bridge, leaning forward over the parapet. Victoria remained motionless. The distant sound of a siren broke what was, for her, a deep silence. The person coughed, retched and spat into the canal below before moving away. She sniffed the air like an animal sensing, whilst she remained motionless. The smell gradually dissipated and the cool of the breeze brought back the more friendly stench of decay. Her heart rate settled as she opened the bottle.

DC Michael Peet tucked his lanyard and ID into his top pocket and searched the room for Skeeter.

'Hoped I'd catch you.' He checked his watch against the clock on the wall. It was just before ten. 'Either I'm early or you're bloody late!'

'Both, my friend. I've nearly done. If I see another black

bloody Range Rover it'll be one too many. You wouldn't believe the paperwork this has generated.'

'Been there, done that.'

Michael Peet was usually on lates. He enjoyed the station when it was not operating at full blast, he could concentrate. As a teenager, he had always wanted to be a lawyer, but his partner's pregnancy in his second year of university had stopped that idea in its tracks. Quickly married, he joined the force and with the arrival of a second, and then a third child, he saw his police career being the one on which he should focus. Working lates also gave him respite from the kids. He had made a five-year plan to return to his studies, but the work he found within Merseyside Police gave him all the challenges he needed. The more mundane the challenge, the greater he enjoyed the work. Finding the needle in the haystack was his speciality, and his determination and ability to see what others could not had helped solve many serious crimes. This skill had been observed by his superiors and his true worth was recognised.

'How are the kids?' Skeeter leaned on her desk.

'Beautiful, but like all kids, they are a drain on my emotions, patience and wallet.'

'But you love them just the same.' Skeeter stood and stretched.

'I love them just the same and more, if I'm honest.' He raised his shoulders. 'No wrestling tonight?' He glanced again at the clock.

'Nope, but looking at the paperwork on your desk you're sure to be, metaphorically speaking of course.' She blew him a kiss. 'Give my love to Joan and the kids.'

* * *

The money in Danny's pocket seemed to burn his thigh. He had resisted all day but the temptation, the draw grew far too strong. It was easier when he was one of the dealers, a little here and there was never missed but then ...

'You're a greedy little shit, Danny.' That's what they had said and they slapped him about a bit. The thought tumbled in his aching head before he spoke. He put on a strong scouse accent, as if he were playing a part on the stage. *'Don't take the piss, like. A little now and then but that's it.'* That was followed by a slap. He remembered the money. Christ there was a lot some nights. They counted it, not once but twice. Sometimes there was a bonus but not always, it depended on who was there. He had never knowingly taken a lot, the same as others, and that not only annoyed but also confused him.

To calm his nerves, he knew what he wanted to buy and where to get it. He needed the crowds; the concert area of the waterfront was a regular haunt.

The Arena area was busy and if he could not locate what he needed there, he needed his backside kicking. Even though it bristled with CCTV, the youthful crowd would ensure the arrival of the back street apothecaries. These dealers knew where the shadows were darkest and could work from within them. Popping out and darting back in, their movements were swift, timed and effective. Like a poacher who has become a gamekeeper, there was a certain instinct. The young dealers were easy to spot, quick to deal and could move on within the blink of an eye. At this point, what he did not want was to meet one of the old gang, not after the last kicking he had received. He moved his hand to his head and caressed the area.

In the corner by the multistorey car park, the vapour from an electronic cigarette ballooned before drifting away. In the darkness stood a young woman, watching and waiting before moving amongst the groups of young people, then soon returning to the same spot. Her hands moved quickly as if by instinct, as goods were exchanged for cash. Nothing seemed to be said but all was understood by nods and simple gestures. Each transaction took only seconds. On one occasion she pretended to be the good Samaritan, by pointing out directions. Danny liked that. He had done it himself on occasion when he feared he was being watched. Moving closer to the shadow, an excitement of anticipation flushed through him. Within seconds the deal was done.

The walk back to his room would take twenty minutes. He called at a corner shop and bought a six pack of Stella, took one and opened it. The cool beer was soothing and boosted his induced mental high. He tossed the empty can to the side and turned away from the river. The uncertainty and concern had evaporated as the chemicals had raced through his bloodstream, the alcohol helping speed the process. Out of nowhere came a bicycle, it passed quickly. Danny paused; the small wheels, the high saddle and red frame caused him to watch it disappear towards the dock road. A tall figure on a small frame brought a smile. He continued, suddenly his mood seemed lighter.

A few minutes later, a booted foot pressed down onto the discarded can crushing it into the pavement; a deliberate act making only the slightest sound. To him, Danny was now a figure in the distance, a dark featureless shape. Within seconds the rider turned right and out of sight.

* * *

Victoria held up the bottle against the orange glow created by the lights along Bankhall Street and squinted to check what remained. There was never enough. 'I could manage another but …' She began to root amongst the cans that were scattered to either side. All were empty. It was then she smelled the cigarette again. This time it was stronger, closer. Struggling, she managed to sit up. She looked immediately at the bridge where the figure had been before. From what she could see in the masking darkness there was no one. The mill chimney on the opposite bank was clearly visible even against the night sky.

'Looking for someone?'

The voice came from somewhere behind her, each word was deliberately emphasised, clear yet almost whispered.

A squeal erupted from deep within her throat echoing within the hollow, covered space, causing the roosting pigeons to flap and fly in panic.

'Who the bloody hell is it and where are you? This is my space, been mine for ages.'

The shriek was shrill and threatening. The birds settled again but they were not fully silent.

'Those flapping wings and your scream make you sound like a harpy, a guardian of the underworld, this world. You need another drink, my girl, as you're supping from an empty bottle as far as I can see in this gloom.'

A bottle landed close to her after bouncing off one of the bags containing her clothing.

'It's full and better quality than the crap you've just had. Take it as a gift from someone who's been where you are right now.'

She glanced at the offering and, even though she could not read the label, the bottle's shape told her just what it was and her fear swiftly dissipated. For a moment she remained still, but her eyes never left the bottle, the smell of cigarette smoke and the intrusion temporarily forgotten.

'Why?' She asked herself, trying to turn her head in the direction in which she believed the bottle had been tossed. There was no answer. Looking back towards the bridge she thought she saw a dark shape move over the parapet wall by the buddleia. *I seem to be surrounded by kindness.* Her thoughts did not linger long and she picked up the latest manna from heaven and unscrewed the top.

* * *

The donor took the steps at the other side of the bridge leading down to the opposite bank of the canal. Turning right, the sanctuary found within the dark shadow beneath the Bankhall Street bridge was perfect. It would take less than an hour for the bottle to be drunk, the contents to an alcoholic were too tempting to savour or to save for rainy days. Pigeons moved along the pipe that traversed the water to the left of the bridgework, the occasional flap of wings hitting the pipe seeming amplified under the archway. It was just after eleven, there were few cars and even fewer pedestrians. If the bottle was empty, neither his return nor the cigarette smoke, nor his action, would trouble her. It was now about being patient.

CHAPTER 5

April twirled the drumsticks as she went through her regular routine. The electronic digital drum kit was spread before her as she accompanied one of her favourite soundtracks. It was the only musical instrument she had been attracted to as a teenager and, shortly after, Tico Torres from the band Bon Jovi, had become her idol. The other Tico in her life lay stretched before the Aga, but he would not rest for long. Moving to the door she collected his lead. His ears pricked and he stood with arching back as he stretched.

The high cirrus clouds streaked the morning blue sky for as far as the eye could see, giving the Irish Sea a pale grey and cold appearance, broken only by the odd white wave top closer to the land. The horizon seemed lost, smudged beyond recognition. April's attention followed Tico as he loped along the sand with a grace and fluidity that only greyhounds seemed to demonstrate. It was a beauty of movement she never tired of.

Gulls called, sharp and deliberate, as they rose from the curving, snake-like strandline set within the wet sand, before landing some distance away. Their flight seemed to tease the dog into a further run. Tico sniffed briefly around the point at which they had alighted, but he did not play their game. After a while he turned and ran back to April before shaking sand from his coat. It was time to leave. Once over the dunes, the house stood back surrounded by the wind-blown pines; there was a stark hostility to their frozen stance. They looked sparse, petrified and dead but they were not. Where the edge of the land met the sea, it had a sinister beauty all of its own. Back at the house, she made coffee and toast. Within half an hour, she would be on her way in to work.

* * *

Arcanum pushed through the misty surface of the Leeds and Liverpool Canal leaving behind a gentle wake on the water's brown surface. The low beat of the engine, like a mechanical heart, echoed from the banks. James Speakman sat at the stern with one hand on the tiller and his other holding a mug of coffee. His eyes focused ahead before they fell on the photograph, trapped behind Perspex and positioned next to the engine gauges. The face he had seen every morning stared back with laughing eyes. James felt the brief mix of emotions, he always did at times like this, before turning his gaze back to the front of the boat and in some ways hoping for a better future. *How long has it been?* The rhetorical question swam in his head. He knew, to the day. He asked himself that same question daily and the number grew by one each time. A heron, legs trailing, flew low ahead of the boat and distracted him from his thoughts; its graceful beauty brought him back to the present.

Travelling at between three and four miles an hour, James knew where each night's stop would be. Considering there were no locks ahead until the Stanley Flight, there were only two low, main swing bridges that needed operating, timing was easy, providing both bridges worked. On occasion, the electrics failed and the guys from the Canal and River Trust had to be called out. If all went well, the boat would make steady progress. His plan that evening was to moor near Aintree. The proximity of the shops and the number of safe mooring locations had made the decision straightforward.

At the end of each day, James cycled along the towpath scouting ahead for the possible locations for the next night's stop. His old folding electric bike made small work of the distances. He was approximately sixteen miles from the Mersey and, to him, the centre of Liverpool.

* * *

'Did you interview Danny Maynard yesterday, Tony?' Skeeter tossed her car keys on the desk.

'He was out. Trying again today. He'll still be in his pit at ten so it will be a pleasure to bring him into the land of the living.' His grin showed a row of teeth. Between each was a light brown stain. If he used a toothbrush, it clearly failed to reach the dental crevices. 'A coffee, check what's on the list, Wicca, and I'm out.' He picked up two pencils and tapped them on top of his computer screen as if playing drums. 'Is our leader joining the fray today or is she over at the new place counting chairs, paper-clips and light bulbs in preparation for the move?' He tapped a drum roll, and then added the crash of a vocal cymbal.

Unbeknown to Tony, April had already entered the room. Skeeter had seen her pause by the door but could do nothing but allow Tony to continue to dig a large hole for himself.

'Was that meant to be a ride cymbal or was it a crash cymbal?' She deliberately emphasised the word *crash*. 'DC Price? You'll definitely know the difference having just watched your dexterity with those HBs. The cymbals each have a different musical inference.'

Tony froze and looked at Skeeter, his face flushed red. Turning to look at April he held up a hand. 'I've no idea, sorry.'

'More like you're on your high horse again, Detective Constable. I warned you before about touching my possessions when I first arrived here. Now let me explain something else.' She looked at Skeeter and moved her head signalling for her to leave. It was understood. She waited a moment as Skeeter left the area. April moved closer. 'May I remind you that I'm your senior officer and if you're going to complain about anyone who you feel might not be pulling their weight, particularly if that person is me, then please have the courtesy to do it to my face and when you do make sure it's in private. Do you understand that instruction?'

Tony nodded and apologised again.

'I want a report on my desk, as soon as, regarding Maynard, and I'd like to see your hair brushed and a degree of polish on your shoes when you return. In the eyes of the public, you represent a professional police force.' She paused allowing her words to sink in. 'Attention to your own personal hygiene forms part of that commitment to our public. When you leave, please tell Skeeter to return.'

Tony Price looked down at his shoes as he tucked her pencils into his top pocket and left.

Skeeter was standing by the top of the stairs checking her phone as he approached. He said nothing, but his face told her all she needed to know.

'Heed whatever was said and act upon it, my friend. She wants the best for you and the team. Something else to remember, Tony, she's good.'

'Thanks! She says you can go back in.' He skipped down the stairs taking two at a time and Skeeter watched him leave. She had grown to like him despite his lack of professional nous.

* * *

The traffic running towards the docks was relatively light. The latest work in preventing vehicles from turning across the main road running parallel to the docks had made a huge difference in maintaining the flow of traffic moving in and out of the city. Once on Regent Road, the main dock walls ran to his right, broken only by occasional castellated gateposts. There was something majestic about their construction: some were regular stone that contrasted with the red brick wall, whilst others were built of tessellated stone, like a vertical jigsaw that seemed to contrast starkly. All had a strength and a distinctive beauty. He remembered Wicca saying they reminded her of the rook pieces on a chess board and he could see just what she meant.

Waterloo Road ran onto Trafalgar Road and his destination, Vulcan Street, appeared on the left. He parked. Although much of the dock area coming from the city had seen a good deal of investment, there were areas where the old had just been burnished but the decay was still visible beneath the cheap veneer. This area was a prime example. The apartments looked fine from above a certain height, but at street level the graffiti artists had been at play. Tony stood momentarily and read what he could decipher, which was very little. Moving towards the entrance, he selected the correct number – four. He pressed the bell and waited. It took a few moments before a faint voice croaked through the damaged speaker.

'Police. DC Price. We've met before on more than one occasion, Danny, we need to chat.'

'One minute.' The buzzing continued for a few moments and then stopped.

After a few minutes the door opened and Maynard looked through the gap. A smell came immediately to Tony's nostrils: a mix of oriental food and damp. The lower portions of the walls clearly reflected where the second smell originated. 'Come up but make sure the door's locked.' There was concern in his voice. Tony followed the instruction. The room, an open plan space comprising kitchen and living room, was sparsely furnished. Through the door in the opposite wall, he could see the unmade bed.

'Sorry to disturb you so early, Danny.' He glanced at his watch; it was just before eleven. 'Good night? How's the head?'

Danny leaned forward to show the wound. Blood still matted his hair that immediately surrounded the gash.

'You've really had your wig split there. I'm no medic, Danny, but that should have been stitched. If it were a metal bar that caused it, a tetanus jab wouldn't go amiss either. People understate the seriousness of that. Lockjaw it's called, as the jaw goes into spasm and then that travels to other parts of the body. They can be so strong, the spasms, they can break bones. Ten percent of people can die from it.'

Danny yawned and looked at Tony. 'You didn't come here to cheer me up by telling me that. What do you want?' There was little respect in his voice.

'Can I sit?' Tony looked at the two-seater settee with mixed feelings.

'No. You'll not be here that long. I'll say again, what do you want?'

'I have two conflicting stories about what happened to you and why you broke into the home of Mr and Mrs Beales.'

'Fuck right off! Who told you I broke in?'

Tony took out his notebook and a pencil from his top pocket. 'Sorry, you approached his door, like I did yours a few moments ago, you knocked or rang the bell and waited patiently. Mr Beales opened the door and invited you in, whilst all along blood spurted from a large gash on the side of your head covering his carpet and furniture when he had welcomed you into his home.'

Danny put his head down and took a deep breath. 'He's a mate, he's known me since I was a kid.'

'Have you ever just walked in before like a large, out-of-control bull?'

He shook his head.

'I agree he's known you a long time. He's also been kind to you. He knows you've not had it easy. Whilst everyone else along that road would be pleased to see you locked up, I can tell that Mr Beales wouldn't. He wants you to just settle down and get a job. He told me the truth about that night as he has no reason to hide or cover any of this up. Someone's out to get even and, from what I know from being in my job a few years, they've only just started.'

Danny went to the kitchen and picked up some cans, but all were empty.

'Why aren't you with your girlfriend and child?'

A can flew across the room and hit the far wall. 'You fucking know, she was shagging my mates when I was inside.'

'And the child?'

'It probably wasn't mine!'

For the first time Tony felt a degree of sympathy for the young man. His life had been moulded by his dissolute parents and a lack of academic achievement. He had read his file. The lad was clearly delusional and had been for some time, believing he was in control, when all along he was dancing to the tune of others.

'If you don't tell me what really happened there's nothing I can do. If you say you fell, then you fell and you're in no danger. If, however, you were attacked, then that's a very different matter.'

Danny leaned on the kitchen worktop, his arms outstretched

and his head down between them. 'I fell and that's an end to the matter.'

'It is, as Mr Beales is not pressing charges for damage to his property. A word to the wise, Danny, don't bring any trouble to the one person who has offered you more than one olive branch. Don't go near and don't lead others to his door. To get to you, they will get to him.'

'Close the front door when you leave.'

'If my gut is to be trusted, Danny, I don't believe I'll be coming back here, unless it's because we are summoned – you're clever enough to understand what that would mean.' He paused, glancing back at Danny, to see if the message had driven home. Tony turned to leave the room before saying, 'One more thing, where's Timbuktu?'

Danny frowned, taken aback by the off-the-cuff question.

'Just asking.'

'Mali, and Mali is in West fucking Africa. Why?'

'No reason. Take great care and watch where you go. You know where I can be found if we can help.'

Tony left the room, took the stairs two at a time before turning the lock on the outside door, and stepped onto the pavement. A deep sigh erupted from his lips as he leaned back to ensure the entrance door had automatically locked. The air seemed to carry the smell of the river as it purged his nostrils. Anything was better than the aroma of the flat.

CHAPTER 6

April studied the recently received autopsy of the suspected suicide. The results were to be expected – high concentration of alcohol in the bloodstream, clear evidence of a long-term drink problem, enlargement of the heart. She read on, not surprised by the details showing the usual skin and hair problems from the lack of washing and exposure to the elements. There seemed little to suggest suicide, with no cause for further investigation. The pathologist's conclusion suggested a combination of self-abuse and age conspiring against a weak will to live. There was no sign of ingestion of a medication. She placed her hands on either side of her face whilst rereading the last part of the report. There would be nothing to investigate other than someone, and gladly it would not be her team, to find and notify his next of kin. From the details discovered so far, it might not be an easy process.

Tony popped his head around the door frame, as he tapped on the architrave. 'Do you have a minute?'

April leaned away from the screen; her thoughts temporarily put on hold. 'You come with news of Maynard?'

Tony nodded and moved into the room. 'Danny Maynard

40

wants no interaction with us at all. He still insists that he fell and he wasn't attacked. I've offered suggestions of what we believe might be waiting for him just around the corner but he still has that arrogance he always demonstrated. He's convinced he's in full control and that his position and value on the streets are higher than they ever could be. If they were, he wouldn't be sporting the serious head injury he is today.'

'He doesn't want to appear to be a grass.' April steepled her fingers and rested her chin on them. 'A worse fate would await anyone who holds that position. Beales, too. He probably prefers to forget the inconvenience of the incident and get on with life without fear of looking over his shoulder every day.' She pointed to the chair by her desk before tapping the computer screen. 'On another note, your vagrant found in the park. We have a name as well as the results from the autopsy. A sad end to a life. It's not considered to be a suicide, neither is it suspicious.'

'What about the medicine bottle?'

April did not respond to the question immediately but offered more information on the victim. 'Felix Spencer, seventy-five years of age and of no fixed address.'

'Our Felix didn't have nine lives then,' Tony mumbled.

'You never know, Tony. There's definitely a past. All someone has to do is find and notify the next of kin. Strangely enough, his personal details were limited and jotted on scraps of paper found in his sock!'

A frown crossed Tony's face. 'Really? I wonder why that was.'

'Well, that's not for you or us to worry about. We have people who do that. He's an import to the area from what we've managed to discover to date. Originally from Brownhills, near Lichfield, where he worked for the Post Office until his retirement. Retired early and sold his home. He had a drink problem even then. Never married. We have a gap in the chronology at this point, until we find that his last known temporary address was in Norbury, Staffordshire. Rental property for only a few months. That was over four years ago. At that point he disappeared again from the radar until you found him. No phone, as far as we know, and no police record. We know that his Post Office pension is directed to a bank account and has not been touched for over twelve years. As it's active and not dormant, there has been no cause for concern, even though it's accruing.'

'What about his state pension?' Tony asked. 'You'd think the bank would ...'

He did not finish on seeing April's expression and hearing her chuckle.

'The answer is yes, and at one time, the bank would be chasing Felix Spencer to advise where to invest his cash, but not now. We're lucky, those using a bank for cash withdrawal are asked if they have plans for the withdrawal owing to fraudulent traders.'

'So, he's disappeared, lived on the streets for a number of years with possibly a considerable amount of money in the bank. Some lucky relatives will be rubbing their hands.' He paused. 'What if there are none?'

'If there are no relatives? I've discovered that the bank will mail the holder for fifteen years and only then, if there's no response, the account will be closed, and the balance sent to RFL Ltd.'

'He could have lived anywhere with two pensions.'

'From what we know, Tony, anywhere within reason, but then he did, for free!"

'Seems strange to me. Something just doesn't add up. Most people would be happy with what he has.'

'Had, Tony, had.' She frowned before adding. 'The medicine bottle? Nothing from it. It is highly unlikely to have belonged to him and was just some litter beneath the bench. As you know there was no label on the bottle. Strange, as I thought all tablets now came in blister packs!'

He raised an eyebrow. 'Not all. Anyway, did you know, as a matter of interest, according to the *Echo*, forty-four homeless people died in Merseyside last year and the average age for men was, I think forty-five and women, forty-three.'

'Drugs and alcohol, Tony.'

'I wonder how many of those were killed?' Tony raised his eyebrows. 'You never know as some are in such a bad state of health.'

April looked at him. 'I think we've enough on our plate as it is, Tony, don't you?'

Tony nodded and left.

She had checked his shoes and it appeared they had seen some kind of polish. All was not lost!

CHAPTER 7

The café was quiet, the last of the late lunchtime trade had left fifteen minutes previously. Lynne sang along to the tune coming from the radio as she disinfected the red patterned Formica topped tables. The sauce bottles and condiments sat on small wooden shelves to the back of the tables, they were clean and ordered and behind them was a laminated menu. Lynne would be leaving in thirty minutes. The owner, Lilian, was in the kitchen cleaning.

'Our usual last customer has not arrived,' Lynne muttered to herself as she removed a dead fly from the windowsill. The green sticker, showing a 'five out of five' star hygiene rating, said much about the café and a great deal more about the dedication of the staff.

Lilian emerged through the beaded screen separating the kitchen from the shop before checking the stock in the counter fridge. 'Looks lovely in here, Lynne, thank you. Another busy one. Has Victoria appeared in her usual casual way like the spectre at the feast pushing her trolley of doom?' They had abbreviated her name to Vicky and received a rebuke – *I was christened Victoria and Victoria I shall be!* – Lilian recalled there was no hostility in her words but a certain pride. It was also clear she was not a scouser nor 'a loser' and that she was, by her use of language, educated.

Lynne checked the clock on the wall and moved to the door. The bell rang as it opened. She checked the three ways in which customers could approach. There was no sign of Victoria.

Lilian pushed the carrier bag holding the polystyrene food containers along the countertop. Prepared for the Trolley Dolly, as she was affectionately known, it had become a ritual that was performed on the six days of the week they were open.

'I can't see her.' Lynne looked genuinely concerned when she moved back inside. 'I do hope she's alright.'

Lilian put a hand to her mouth to suggest she was drinking. 'Maybe late owing to a little distraction. I'm here for another hour so she has time. I'll hang the bag on the shutter if she doesn't arrive before I go. You've done enough for one day, love, you go, and I'll see you tomorrow.'

Lynne slipped off her apron and grabbed her coat. 'Thanks, see you.'

The bell on the door rattled as she left. Within ten minutes she was on Bankhall Street and a further ten would see her on Stanley Road and five minutes from home. As she approached the canal, she saw the shopping trolley and, more significantly, she noticed the drooping Eeyore strapped to the front. The trolley was empty. Lynne moved to the bridge and looked down at the canal. The sun shone on the rippling surface adding an animated pattern to the gable of the building. Moving nearer to the end of the bridge, she had a clear view into the derelict loading area, and she could also see some bags.

'Victoria!' The word seemed to bounce off the structures. Pigeons immediately took flight, the flapping of their wings making them sound bigger than they were. Lynne called again, only louder. 'Victoria, it's Lynne from the café. Are you there?'

'Are you all right, love. Have you lost a cat, like?' The rich scouse accent was warm and friendly but it startled her. A middle-aged man dressed in overalls stood to her right. Lynne giggled feeling a little embarrassed.

'That trolley belongs to a lady who, we believe, lives on the streets. I know it's hers because of Eeyore strapped to the front. Some bags down there may be hers. We give her food every day we're open, and for the first time in absolute ages, she didn't turn up today. I hope she's okay.'

'I'll check if you want.'

Lynne nodded quickly. 'Please, thank you, that would stop me worrying. She's such a sweet old thing.'

Moving to the bridge parapet, he looked over. Some of the finer branches of the buddleia had been broken and the grass below had been recently trampled on; he could see the faint pathway that had been worn. 'Looking at that, she must use this route daily.'

Sliding over the coping stone, he lowered himself to the grass that was barely a metre below and kept to the edge of the building. Despite being close to industry, roads and the railway, the lapping of the canal against the bank seemed to whisper and bring a peace and tranquillity. It was an immediate haven of calm. Within five strides he saw the shoes. Both feet faced upwards forming an angle at the heels. Leaning further forward, he could see the blanket and then the body propped against pallets and the many surrounding plastic bags. The body was that of a woman. Her mouth gaped and her hair semi-covered her face. An empty bottle and a number of cans were scattered on what appeared to be a makeshift bed as well as the ground around her, whilst another bottle was still in her hand.

'Fuck me!' His words were rushed and he instinctively moved his body back whilst his feet remained planted. 'Victoria!' The shout seemed louder, trapped beneath the roof that formed the hollow space. There was no response and the last thing he wanted to do was go any closer. Holding his hands to his mouth he tried again, this time louder.

'Have you found her? Is she alright?' Lynne spoke with an eagerness as he returned. He jumped, placing one hand on the bridge top while the other grabbed the buddleia as he scrambled up and over. He said nothing until he was on the pavement.

'I think so but ...'. He had already removed his mobile and tapped in 999.

'I knew something was wrong. I told Lilian.' She began to weep whilst throwing her arms around the stranger. 'I didn't know her personally but she came every day. She had a lovely smile and was always grateful and seemed happy. She's someone's mother, grandmother. How can her relatives allow her to get into this dreadful state?'

The stranger moved back a step and held her at arm's length. 'What's your name?'

'Lynne.' She wiped her tears with her sleeve.

'My name is John, Lynne. Some people make the life they want and that can be in total contrast to that of our own. Sometimes we're swift to judge because of that difference. She might have been happy with her lot. She could have lived in an abusive relationship, lost her family. Not everyone wants family. You said yourself she always seemed happy and had a ready smile. That tells you a lot and you and your friend Lilian were good Samaritans. You helped rather than rejected her, she felt safe coming to you, and you were obviously touched by her.'

The siren drowned the everyday noises and the blue lights swiftly moved up Bankhall Street. Lynne turned to look and then turned her eyes to John. 'Thank you for all you've done and said.'

John raised a hand and moved to the kerbside as the

approaching police car pulled in. The siren was silenced but the blue strobes remained blinking. The two officers emerged.

'She's over the wall in the derelict loading area. I think she's dead but I didn't get too close. I'm John and this is Lynne. I just stopped to help, like.'

The first officer looked at Lynne and nodded to his colleague who took her to the car to sit down. He remained with her.

'I went over here. That's her trolley. Lynne works at the café at the bottom of the road and they make sure the woman has the food they have left at the end of the day. She said her name's Victoria.'

The officer peered over the wall and then towards the building.

'She's lying on a mattress and some pallets. I called her name a few times but there was no response. Her mouth is gaping, but you can't see her face proper owing to her hair, it's dangling forward.'

A second siren could be heard coming from a different direction. All heads turned as the noise grew. A first responder paramedic vehicle rounded the corner and stopped in front of the police car. There followed a brief explanation. Securing a red rucksack, the paramedic slipped over the parapet and made his way along the short stretch of canal bank. Within ten minutes, he returned and stood just below the wall. He shook his head. 'I can confirm she's dead . There doesn't appear to be foul play but looking at the amount of alcohol consumed and her age, she looks like another statistic.' Handing the rucksack to the officer he swiftly climbed over and onto the pavement.

* * *

Skeeter nipped the dying head off one of the flowers near the path leading to the front door of her cottage. Roby Mill was quiet apart from the occasional wagon powering up Bank Brow coming from the quarry on Lees Lane. It was the only downside to living in the village. She chuckled to herself as she remembered someone mentioning that there was even a snake in the garden of Eden so nowhere could be perfect.

'Are you chuckling to yourself, Skeeter?' Tom's voice startled her. He was standing on the other side of the hedge.

'Didn't smell the smoke, Tom. Been spying on me long?' She chuckled again as she peered over the edge.

'Nope. Early evenings are my thing. Love the peace and the bird song. Early finish for you, young lady?'

She checked her watch; it was just before seven. It was then that she saw the smoke rise, grey wisps curling before disappearing, leaving behind a delicate aroma. 'My normal shift. Worked well over, yesterday. You didn't miss me, I see.'

'A policeman's lot is not a happy one ...' He sang the words, but not in tune. He paused to cough. 'Should really give these up before they ruin my voice completely.'

'When constabulary duty is to be done,' Skeeter responded. 'Funnily enough, Tom, I was in the cast for *The Pirates of Penzance* when I was in school. I guess the writing was on the wall that I might join the constabulary.'

She heard the click of the gate and looked towards the road. 'It's the flying squad, Tom.'

'Looks nothing like Regan or Carter if you ask me. Boyfriend, is he?'

'Part of our Drone Unit. Plays with drones and gets paid for the privilege. Just a friend, but you never know.'

'Another one with a bobby's job. Handsome young fella though.'

Steve waved and walked down the path. 'I'm early. Parked by the pub. Are you ready?'

Skeeter rubbed her hands together and he stopped. He saw

the top of Tom's head on the opposite side of the hedge. 'Steve this is my neighbour, Tom. He keeps an eye on me and the house. He's probably assessing you as we stand here. You chaps have a chat and I'll go and powder my nose.'

'What?' Both men spoke in unison.

'Euphemism boys, euphemism!'

The restaurant was quiet. Skeeter stared at the large gin and tonic. 'How's Matrix?'

'I believe you'll be coming over in a short while. I can assure you, it's a better environment to the one you're in now. Makes sense bringing everyone under the one roof.'

'Eggs in one basket can have devastating consequences, my mother used to say. Cheers. It's lovely to see you. No more shop talk.'

Steve laughed. 'If you can manage it, then I feel sure so can I.'

CHAPTER 8

Steve left Skeeter's cottage early. The dawn had just broken over the valley. The ripped red and orange colours brought an unusual hue to the rest of the awakening sky. The sharp, piercing cawing of rooks in far trees made him look their way. Closing the front door, he stood momentarily enjoying the cool freshness of the air.

'Morning, Steve. Just a word if you don't mind, as a friend of a dear friend. Don't harm the lass. She means a lot to me and the missus.' Tom was never one to shy away from saying what he meant.

Steve could again only see the top of his balding head and responded in his direction. 'I've no intention of doing that, Tom. Have a good day and nice to meet you. Let's hope that next time I can put a face to a name and voice.' He moved up the path, and on closing the gate, he looked back. Skeeter waved from the upstairs window. Strangely, Tom also waved from his door. He was even smaller than Steve had envisaged. Checking his watch, Steve had just enough time to get to his flat and then to Speke.

The morning briefing at Copy Lane was a regular daily event and was, as the title implies, a brief, informal round-up of what had transpired between shifts and what needed to be done in the forthcoming hours. There was also the need to manage any absences as well as keeping the team abreast of the planned move.

DC Kasum Kapoor had arrived early and waited for the other members of the team. April was next, along with Lucy, who bubbled with an eagerness for the end of the day as she was to begin a week's leave. They prepared coffee and chatted. Michael had gone home, but as usual, he had left a note attached to April's computer screen. He called it his daily epistle and the messages varied in length depending on the specific tasks set. It had become a habit, blending dedicated police work with friendly banter. April looked forward to reading them, it made a change to see a non-digital communication.

'I see we have another death.' Kasum commented. 'This time, it's a homeless woman. Two in a few days is two too many. I know it's not unusual in such a large city but the weather hasn't been too inclement. Sometimes I—'

'Morning!' Skeeter bounced into the room a broad smile etched across her face. 'Coffee, I could murder a coffee.' The word 'murder' seemed to reinforce Kasum's point as she looked at April, Lucy and then towards Skeeter.

'Cat got the cream, Miss Warlock?' April waited, but did not expect an answer and so was not disappointed at the lack of Skeeter's response, nor did she pursue it.

April brought the coffee over as Tony came in. He was neither bouncing nor enthusiastic. His greeting was a simple grunt as he headed for the kettle.

April moved to her desk and glanced at the note Michael had left but decided she would read it after the briefing. 'The handover this morning suggests they had a busy night, but one area on which we need to focus immediately is this. Control received a call from Danny Maynard.' She found the recording of the 999 call. There was the sound of heavy breathing, followed by a few gasps, before broken speech emerged:

'Jesus – again!' More heavy breathing and a groan. *'Help! Must move and hide from these bastards they're going to – hide, Dan, fucking hide and get rid of it ... I know you can track where I am ... you need to find ...'*

The call ended abruptly.

'Mobile phone tower triangulation placed the location of this call to the area around the Parish Church and was timed at 23.37. Since then, the phone has been dead.'

'Maybe he was heading for the church garden, he's either entering from Chapel Street and the Old Church Yard – there are large bins along the side of the garden where he might have been trying to conceal himself – or he could have come from George's Dock Gates. I'm not sure if that route is closed after a certain time.' As he spoke Tony immediately sat up as if he had suddenly come alive. 'What's he getting rid of?'

'The Homeless Jesus statue.' Kasum's words were almost a whisper but April immediately picked up on them.

The church gardens situated next to the Parish Church held a number of bronze statues and memorials, one of which was a statue of a reclining homeless person depicting Jesus wrapped in a blanket.

'The area was searched but he wasn't there, nor was there anything to suggest he had been at that location. Nothing was found. They carried out another search at first light, still nothing, but they did find what they believe to be a trail of blood near the church wall. They're checking CCTV from the area and that shouldn't take long to come through, Tony.'

'His accommodation?' Tony asked. There seemed to be real concern in his voice.

'Nothing. He's not returned and nor has he gone to his

uncle's place. Beales hasn't contacted us to say he'd seen him so we're assuming he's not there.

'No further calls from him, I take it?' Skeeter leaned on the desk.

'Nothing.'

'Speaking of the homeless, another report has come in detailing the death of another vagrant. It's the discovery of another body, this time female and according to the woman who found her, she was known as Victoria. Apparently, Victoria was fed on a daily basis through the benevolence of Lil's Café near the dock road. According to the report, Victoria called late every afternoon to collect any food that was left or close to its sell-by date. Post-mortem examination will no doubt show alcohol and age-related death. There's always that pattern whether it be drugs, booze or the cold.'

Kasum jotted down a few notes and it was clear from her expression something was bothering her.

'Thanks all. We have our tasks and I have to see DCI Mason.'

The group began to disperse. 'Kasum, I'd love to look into Victoria's death but it's not for us, I'm sorry, I know how concerned you are.'

Kasum nodded and mouthed the words, *thank you* as she left. April turned to Tony.

'Tony, chase the CCTV images for last night and act accordingly, but keep me informed. Danny is feral and a survivor, but somehow, I feel, and I'm sure you do too, the odds are stacked heavily against him.'

'Thanks, ma'am.' Tony's words were most sincere.

She had not experienced this degree of interest in him since her arrival at Copy Lane. It was reassuring to see he had the fire for policing even though his appearance seemed to negate that impression. *You can't judge a book* ... Her thought was interrupted as she took Michael's note from the screen:

April,

Good morning. I hope your evening went well and the team is firing on all cylinders.

The files you requested are sorted and dispersed as per instruction. However, rather than have a break, I took the opportunity to review the post-mortem of the vagrant found in Hesketh Park. I was fascinated by the findings, the when, where and how he died, but not forgetting the need to identify the deceased, a task which proved difficult in this case. The report reveals how they, from the evidence garnered, believe the person died. It's their conclusion about the cause of death. Remember also, cost will be a lead factor. I noted that owing to the lack of suspicious circumstances, it was initially believed to be a suicide, but the pathologist reports his findings to be death through a combination of alcohol, age and chronic heart failure. There was clear evidence seen after inspecting the liver and kidneys and of course, the heart. There was a note to show high potassium content in the blood tests and I assume that only a limited toxicology test was run owing to the strength of the evidence mentioned.

I did a little digging after reading the file. Immediately questions were posed but the main one was why did he retain the small collection of papers noting certain personal details? Another thing, why were they wrapped in plastic and kept in his sock? The information has no real significance to anyone, or does it? It is my belief that he was running from something and I feel there's more to this death than meets the eye, considering the broad and disparate evidence we have at present. I'm going to use my free time to find answers – eat and work, you might say. I hope that meets with your approval.

Getting a second PM will be impossible unless the request can be supported by more evidence.

When you read this, I will be in the land of dreams.

Michael

April smiled at the formality of the handwritten note. She paused and read it again. 'There's no harm, Michael, providing it's done in your time.' She spoke out loud, to no one.

* * *

Tony pulled into the parking area of Canning Place, the old headquarters that was still partially in use, most of the services having made the move to Rose Hill. The transition was seen as not only a technological improvement with better staff welfare, specialised forensic suites and facilities, but also there was to be a huge financial saving. The cynical might argue that Canning Place was perfectly placed as a piece of real estate to reap a high financial reward. With Matrix at Speke, Rose Hill and Edge Lane, the main motor transport hub, all were new, purpose-built facilities. The Merseyside force was well placed to move forward in the fight against the constantly changing face of crime and the criminal world.

Even though the sun was out, there was a decided chill coming from the river. Looking across at the Albert Dock made him proud of the city and, in particular, the waterfront. Some of the more modern buildings had split public opinions, but as a young man he believed strongly that things could not remain in the past. Modern architecture should play a part in fashioning the city.

Strand Street, the main two-lane thoroughfare separating the Mersey from the heart of the city, was busy. Pausing, he viewed the rear of the Three Graces – the Liver, the Cunard and the Port of Liverpool buildings – all magnificent and situated on the

Pier Head. No matter how often he passed, he needed just a moment to appreciate their grandeur.

Within minutes, he was standing at the stairs on George's Dock Gates, the stone steps that would lead him to the church gardens, the place from where they believed Danny had made the call the previous night. Tony took them two at a time, two flights of ten. He paused on reaching the top and breathed out. A few pedestrians were making their way through the paths and some were sitting and enjoying the morning sunshine, whilst being partially sheltered from the cooling river breeze.

The Blitz monument immediately caught his eye. There were dark stains close to the base, possibly signs of blood, but there was little guarantee, and if it were blood it might not be Danny's. The bronze figure of a small boy holding a model aircraft whilst standing on the top step of a spiral staircase, his arm outstretched, made him reflect on his own childhood and his love of aviation. Considering the meaning of the monument, there was an innocence in the pose, and in particular the expression on the child's face. Turning, he followed the dark spatter-like markings on the stone path. It was clear that whoever had left them had paused occasionally as greater concentrations of spotting were visible. The Homeless Jesus statue was his next port of call. The concealed figure, with only feet and a small section of the face exposed, lay on a bench. Small bits of rubbish, paper and cigarette butts, had collected beneath and the occasional gust twirled them briefly into life before they changed places and settled again.

'Where are you, Danny Boy and why here of all places?' Tony's words were but a whisper yet they were heard by an elderly gent sitting to his right.

'Are you alright, lad?' The words were sincere. 'You lost something or someone?'

'You might say that.' He stared briefly at the man and then

turned three-hundred-and-sixty degrees taking in the whole garden. 'A friend was here late last night, birthday celebration, and he lost a phone,' Tony lied. 'I work down the road and said I'd pop up to check, but I can't see it.'

'A lot of people have come through here today and if anyone's found it, they might have handed it in at the church. It's open now. Not all scousers nick what's not nailed down!' The old man chuckled. 'Otherwise, Jesus there would have lost his blanket.'

Tony laughed and thanked the man. 'I'll check and do one more sweep.'

He walked to the church. The electric doors slid open, seeming incongruous and anachronistic. He made the enquiry, but he knew that the likelihood of Danny leaving a phone was improbable. A mobile would be a lifeline to a drowning man and right now, as far as Tony saw it, he was in perilous water. Besides, the idea of leaving his phone was probably a lie and he wondered why he had pursued the tale. On leaving the church, his own phone vibrated as he worked his way past the bins and three parked motorcycles.

'We have some stills taken from CCTV of the green space by the church. It looks like your chap, Maynard. He approaches from Chapel Street onto The Old Churchyard before entering the garden proper. He squats by one of the benches and looks to make a call. He's still on the phone when he moves towards the church. He stops on a couple of occasions before standing by a tall statue close to some stone steps and a fence.'

Tony looked at the Blitz memorial. 'I know where that is. Go on.'

'He pauses, jumping up and climbing the fence before disappearing. Within minutes of his leaving, three more people can be seen rushing in and immediately searching the area. I'll send a link.'

'As far as I can see, there are three cameras looking onto this place. Do you have images from all three?'

'Working on it.'

Tony waited to receive the details. It took only moments. He studied the grainy black-and-white footage, glancing in the direction of the camera he believed had taken the images. He ran the video over three times, pausing it at the moments when Danny had stopped. He checked each location in turn but found nothing apart from the dark spatter. Maybe Danny had made up the story like he had so many in the past. Maybe his assumption was correct, and all this was bullshit. The alert told him another message had arrived. It was more video footage. Checking the angle, he looked for the camera and swiftly located it. The images were clearer, but not much. He sat this time to watch the whole video. He then looked around the garden, focusing on the bell positioned on a filigree metal stand. 'He gave us a bell last night.' His thoughts seemed illogical yet at the same time …

Tony checked every part of the low structure but found nothing. A gull called from over by the Liver Building, it seemed closer, shrill and urgent, like a warning.

'You!' The man to whom he had spoken earlier pointed to the Blitz memorial.

Tony turned and saw him approach, his arm still pointing at the statue.

'I think there's something on the step next to the top by the centre column. The movement of the sun seemed to bring light to that area. It was in shadow before. I was looking for the gull.'

Moving across, Tony reached the level indicated and with a handkerchief in hand, he collected the object he knew to be a phone. 'Bloody hell! Can you believe that?'

'My words exactly, lad. Your friend will be over the moon. Damn strange place to lose it if he were walking through here.' He turned to leave shaking his head.

'Thanks, you've saved the day.'

The man lifted a hand.

The forensics suite at Rose Hill Headquarters would take time to analyse the phone digitally. It was time Tony could not afford and certainly, any delay tracking Maynard, might prove fatal.

Within forty minutes, Tony was back in the office.

CHAPTER 9

A thin veil of smoke drifted from the boat's chimney. There always seemed to be a breeze along the canal, coming in various degrees of strength dependent on the time of day, the season or a combination of both. What it always was, however, was unpredictable. James tried to think of the last occasion on which there was none, when the day dawned flat and still, but he could not. What he did know was that if there was no wind, then there would be a mist or fog lying low, grey and smothering all along the waterway. If he had the choice, he would take the breeze. Fog brought a dampness and a certain claustrophobia and he did not appreciate that, he had suffered enough in a past life when personal responsibility trapped a free spirit.

He grabbed the metal poker to stir the wood in the belly of the stove before he brought his hand to touch the side of the kettle. It was barely warm. 'I'm not watching you, honest, so you can hurry up and boil.'

The battery radio was set to Radio Merseyside; the music held little interest; he was waiting for the weather forecast. The unopened bottle of whisky sat on the table in front of him where he had put it when he moved through the boat. It was his game, his morning challenge, his fight against the evil that was trapped within like some golden manic genie. He had played this game every day for four years, four months and thirteen days, and so far, the genie had remained imprisoned within the glass.

'Today's weather forecast until noon ...' The report allowed his focus to change.

James's shoulders relaxed as he listened before collecting the bottle and placing it back in the cupboard. The following day the challenge would begin again. The whistle from the kettle, a welcome intrusion, meant the morning could truly begin.

* * *

Tony removed some of the notes and images that were attached by coloured magnets from the boards that formed a ninety-degree angle to the side and back of his workspace. He had added a small street map of the area, stretching from the outer docks at Crosby to beyond Liverpool centre and drawn a circle around the location of Danny's accommodation and that of the parish church garden. Surrounding the map he had added pictures of the buildings and items within the garden, as well as a hand-written note of the transcript of the last call Danny had made.

Further CCTV footage had been assessed, indicating that he had crossed Strand Street and taken the road towards the Crowne Plaza, an area bristling with CCTV cameras. Once there, he had many options to keep him lost within the shadows. From what Tony saw, it might be assumed that he was looking for somewhere to hide, settle, recover and think, somewhere away from the main roads. As Tony stood with his hands on his head studying the boards, a paper dart flew over his left shoulder before stubbing its nose against the wall.

Skeeter grinned from the side of her computer screen. 'You

should go in for window dressing. Very pretty. If that's all you have to do with your time ...'

Bending, he collected the paper plane and unfolded it to reveal what he expected to be a written sarcastic comment. He read it:

I'd talk to Beales. He knows more than he's letting on in my opinion. Why shield someone unless you have something to hide?

He folded the paper back to resemble the aircraft before picking up a magnetic disc and attaching it to the board. 'Like what, Wicca?'

'If you study Danny's record, there have been three checks on his uncle's property when it was believed Danny was stashing drugs there, along with a stolen quad and motorbikes. Often having these items can be a clear link within the process of distribution, as well you know. The bikes were found and removed but no drugs were discovered.' She held up a piece of paper detailing a report of the search. 'After the first occasion, you'd be a bloody fool to stash nicked items there and yes, I know, Danny is a bloody fool, but he's not a stupid, bloody fool. My guess is, Tony, our Mr Beales, who by his own admission has a soft spot for the lad, might just have helped him a little too much.'

Tony tapped the now pinned paper aircraft that resembled the start of a lepidopterist's collection. 'Danny has, we hope, survived the night, providing he's not already floating through the mouth of the Mersey, as I speak. He's going to need a friend, he's going to need cash and both of those needs are also in short supply. When they're in his position, these people never attract many friends. He's left his girlfriend. He was told she was shagging his so-called mates when he was inside.'

'See Beales and find out if, in the past, Danny asked him to look after anything when he went away. Also ask if Danny has a key to any part of his property.'

'Thanks, Wicca.'

'Don't thank me, Tony, thank god you know me.' She winked and ducked back behind her screen.

* * *

April sat before DCI Mason. The main agenda had been covered, finalising the essential details in preparation for the team's move to the new location. She had also presented a swift assessment of the performance of each member of the team, before the conversation turned to the increased number of homeless deaths. Ordinarily, this would not be discussed at this level, as it was known from the statistics that some years saw an increase above the norm.

'Just keep a watching brief, April. Monitor if there are others. I'm aware, as with suicide cases, murder can be masquerading under the smokescreen. There's been nothing untoward with either post-mortem, I take it. I'm assuming a coroner's officer attended both scenes?'

'We believed the first to be but were proved wrong on that assumption. It wasn't, according to the pathologist, a drug overdose. Apart from that, both victims met the same criteria: alcohol, homelessness and old age. There was, according to the limited toxicology tests carried out, higher than normal potassium concentration in the bloods.'

Mason frowned. 'And the reason?'

'The report shows poor kidney function in both, plus a heavy and prolonged dependency on alcohol, suggesting the reason both suffered from hyperkalemia. The evidence, and there was none to highlight suspicious circumstance, points to, or indicates, alcohol and long-term abuse.'

'No witnesses or next of kin?' Mason stood, suggesting the meeting was coming to an end.

'We know one died intestate yet had money from two pensions still coming into a bank account. We've not managed to trace any relatives or next of kin, but we've run requests for help within the press and on our socials. I'm assuming we'll have the same difficulties with Victoria. We don't even have a surname for her as yet. There will be DNA taken and, as per procedure, tissue samples and body fluids analysis will be held. It will soon be out of our hands.'

'Looking forward to having you here under the one roof.' Mason opened the door and smiled. 'Keep me informed.'

* * *

James sat back and smoked the roll up as *Arcanum* plodded gently along, following the watery scar that at that moment ran through the countryside to his right. Rimrose Valley Country Park stretched well ahead, yet at this point it was mostly hidden by the trees lining the water's edge; it was natural, green and in total contrast to the opposite bank that was filled with houses. Coming into any city or town, James often experienced a sense of claustrophobia, an anxiety that had grown more intense with age. It was a feeling that made him defensive and cautious as to where he should moor the boat and whether to leave it unattended. His scouting sessions helped to alleviate some of that worry. The idiom, forewarned is forearmed, seemed to be a mantra relevant to this situation and he had lived by it for some time. Making the decision on the next mooring point was no exception. He had identified an old spur in Bootle, set to the right of the main canal route. It was, he assumed, once an industrial building, now demolished; he had used it once before. Most of the area was only partially rebuilt; apartments filled one side yet the other was secured with fencing prior to further development.

He inhaled the last drag from what was left of the cigarette and tossed it overboard; it was soon lost in the boat's wake. Returning his gaze to the front, he gave another cursory glance at the face trapped behind the transparent layer. 'For you, I do this for you. I hope you know that.'

* * *

Beales was out but his wife welcomed Tony into the house. He accepted the offer of a coffee. His old boss had insisted that accepting a drink would help settle those who were to be interviewed. Wayne Beales was at work. Mrs Beales brought in the drinks and biscuits. She was certainly an attractive woman. 'These were always Danny's favourites when he was little.' She laughed. 'I still keep them in, must be a habit. Hopefully, we won't see much of him after the last episode.'

'I hope he's all right, Mrs Beales. You won't know about this but he was attacked again and he's missing. He could be—'. Tony had deliberately adapted his voice to sound frightened for the lad and did not finish the sentence, hoping to elicit a response.

She was about to put the mug to her lips when she stopped. 'I think he came here last night.'

'Go on.' Tony sat up. The fish had taken the bait.

'It was late. Well, I assumed it to be him. Wayne was up watching something on the TV like he always does. I woke to hear voices and thought it sounded like Danny and not something on the telly.'

'How long was he here?' Tony sat forward.

'I don't know. I drifted off. I take a tablet, you see, to help me sleep. I can't understand why I woke in the first place.'

'Did you ask Wayne about it this morning?'

'He leaves before I get up – earlies, his favourite shift for some reason. The medication's fault. If it were him, I know he didn't have anything to eat or drink as everything was tidy, if he had, the dishes would've been in the sink. Doesn't do clearing and washing, my husband. Doesn't do much at all if I'm honest.'

Tony did not reply for a moment, hoping she would say more but he could sense a deep resentment in her eyes.

'He still works and I suppose I should be thankful for that. Neither does he piss his wages against the wall every night nor bet on the horses.' She smiled.

'Indeed, Mrs Beales. He works at T. P. Jones Foods in Bootle?'

'Yes, as I said, he's been on earlies this last few weeks. That's his preferred shift. *Off the couch and into work*, as he often says. For some reason, he's managed to wrangle a few weeks on earlies.'

Tony thanked her for the coffee and her honesty before informing her that the police were doing all they could to find and protect Danny from further harm.

'Officer.' Mrs Beales touched his arm.

Tony turned to look at her.

'Please don't tell Wayne I've told you. Please! He can be … you know, a bit funny sometimes if he thinks I said something I shouldn't.'

'Thank you. Don't worry.' Tony did not expand. He nodded and smiled before returning to the car.

* * *

The reception area of T. P. Jones was attractive. A large yucca plant sat in one corner, the leaves a deep, rich green. The wall displayed framed photographs of the processes taking place within the factory itself. The receptionist had immediately responded on seeing his warrant card by personally asking a member of the management team to escort Wayne to the front office. Tony had refused the offer of a drink.

'Come this way, DC Price. It's private in the boardroom and a little more comfortable.'

The small office he entered was not what he had envisaged, but it was light and clean and almost a replica of the reception. Wayne came in a few moments later, immediately recognising Tony. His expression changed, believing the worst.

'Is everything alright?'

'Please sit.' Tony intended to let Beales stew a little.

'Is it Danny?' He pulled a chair from the table and sat. There was genuine concern on his face.

Tony sat back and folded his hands before momentarily resting his chin on them. He presented his warrant card. 'You know what that is, Mr Beales?'

Beales nodded.

'I could caution you. That doesn't mean arrest you but it ensures what you say should be the whole truth. There's a serious implication to my being here and I know that you know what that might be.'

The noise from somewhere in the building could be heard as neither spoke for a few moments. Tony could almost see the workings inside Wayne's head as the contorted confusion became clearly etched on his face.

'Danny?'

Tony nodded returning his hands beneath his chin.

'Is he all right, like?' Beales muttered with anxiety in his voice.

'When did you last see him? Please think carefully before you answer.'

'He came to the house last night. Have you been speaking to …'

Tony held up a finger. 'Just answer my questions. Let's not

speculate where this information comes from at this stage. Now, carry on.'

'I was just nodding off on the couch, I do that when I'm on earlies, so I can get out without waking the wife. Danny tapped on the window. I'd locked the door as you suggested. He had blood down his face, but it wasn't as bad as before. He'd managed to get away but he knew they'd be looking for him. He said he needed my help, money and somewhere to stay, to lay low. Can you believe that after the last episode? Somewhere to fucking stay! Bloody hell, the kid's not normal, not proper normal, any road.'

'What time was this?'

'About two.'

'That was late. What did you do?'

'I keep a hundred quid in a tin, rainy day money, I call it. I gave him that, an old sleeping bag and a rucksack. I remember I also gave him a small bottle of brandy. I told him to fuck off and not come back as he'd bring the problem and those looking for him to me and the missus if he already hasn't done so. I didn't sleep, just kept listening thinking I might suddenly get unwanted company. The people he deals with can be bloody cruel bastards, you said that, and I've heard it before. They take no prisoners if they feel they've been betrayed or that you're hiding something from them ...'

'Very cruel. I've witnessed it, I've seen them cut and stab someone ninety times but not kill them. They want to make sure the others who follow will see, learn a lesson and fear. Something else, too. It doesn't matter who you are. If you get in their way, stop them from achieving what they've set out to do ... the consequences can be ... but you know that.'

'Thanks, I was already a nervous bag of crap before you came here.'

'Has he ever asked you to hide anything for him? Ever?' Tony leaned forward. 'The truth and the whole truth.'

Beales lowered his head.

'What was it and when?'

'This is going to sound so bloody stupid. He asked me to look after a box.' He mimicked the dimensions with his hands.

'A substantial box, then?'

'Yes, but it wasn't as heavy as I thought it would be. He told me it was a surprise for his uncle for being so kind. Asked my missus if she'd wrap it, you know, with proper paper and a ribbon, and she did. He retrieved it one evening and a taxi collected him from the top of my drive. It wasn't for his uncle at all.'

'Anything else?'

Another pause ensued and a second lowering of the head. 'I let him use my shed. I think he used it when I was on lates or in bed. There was never anything out of place but I knew he'd been in.'

'Did he stash anything?'

Beales raised his shoulders. 'It was how I left it. Bit of a bomb site if I'm honest, but I tend to know where things are or if things have been moved.'

'You felt sorry for him?'

'You're right, I did. I told you. He had nothing as a child other than good hidings.'

'He's gone missing. He called the police. He was scared. You assured me you would call me no matter what time if he were to turn up. You didn't. That lack of a simple phone call might have cost him dearly. For your sake, and that of the lad, let's hope not.'

'He was safe until about five when I dropped him off before I came in to work.'

'Where?'

'Brasenose Road. He went down Bedford Place, there's a

bridge that crosses the canal. He told me he was going to walk down the towpath. As I said, he had a sleeping bag and stuff.' He looked at the expression on DC Price's face and then at his hands. 'I just thought that was best for him. To keep him safe.'

'He's still missing and the one thing he isn't, Mr Beales, is safe. Make sure you keep yourself secure. Stop putting yourself in potential harm's way and let us help you, as in that way, you might just help him. You have my number.'

CHAPTER 10

The officer sat in the café; she had been instructed to glean any information about Victoria. The coffee before her was a welcome offering. She could sense from the café owner that the discovery had affected both herself and her colleague.

'If I were honest with myself,' Lilian ran her finger around her mug, 'I wasn't shocked on hearing the news. I'd been aware of Victoria's physical condition and I'd witnessed a gradual deterioration in her appearance over the time since she'd been calling. You'd expect that for someone living on the streets and considering her age. That's why we're charitable, officer, you can immediately see where your donation is going and we know it's not going to some charity director who earns thousands. Besides, I was always taught, charity begins at home, so it's the least we can do. It's not the way someone of her age should die in my opinion, not with the welfare system we have.'

'Did you know anything about her?'

'No, not really. She liked an egg and bacon butty over sausage but I'm sure that's not what you meant.' The words brought a smile that swiftly faded. 'It was my belief she was quite a sophisticated woman – the way she spoke, her politeness

– there was just something about her, a pride you might say. Did you know she still wore makeup? She might not have washed regularly but she always wore her lippy. I also believe she was disappointed in what she'd become and I think she saw herself as pathetic. Maybe that's why she had Eeyore tied to her trolley.'

'Did she mention where she was originally from or a surname?'

Lilian shook her head. 'No. When she first appeared, she told me and Lynne she'd once lived in a detached house in the country, Cheshire way, and had driven a swanky car, those weren't her exact words. Life, she said, could be unpredictable and you could make one too many mistakes and before you knew it – it had all gone!'

The officer continued making frantic notes.

'It was the way she said it. There was no sadness, no remorse when she spoke. She always thanked us and told us we were very kind, that we would be rewarded one day. Funnily, on reflection, she would also say that she'd wished she'd been kinder when she'd had the chance.' Those words brought with them a reverent silence, broken only by the ring from the doorbell. Lilian glanced at the customer before turning back. 'Will there be a funeral?'

'If no next of kin can be found it's likely to be a pauper's funeral.'

Lilian shook her head. 'Didn't know they still existed. That would be so sad. Can you let us know? We'd like to attend. I'd close the café. One or two of the lads who call in here for late lunch knew her – they called her, *The Queen.*'

* * *

The digital forensic report had come back and the prints on the phone were evidence that Danny had handled it. Further touch

DNA tests were being processed. Tony stared at the three saved numbers; everything else had been deleted and then the SIM card had been destroyed. However, they certainly were not looking at a phone linked to the Encrochat, the sophisticated global criminal communication system, but something far more naïve. This, it was felt, was his personal 'business' phone. It would have been a waste of time had it not been for their ability to open a link to cloud storage, the disappointment being it contained only thirteen photographs which had been retrieved and enhanced.

Bloody thirteen, just my luck. His thoughts at least brought a chuckle. *Unlucky for some? Unlucky for me!*

The photographs were a mismatch. He spread them on the desk in no particular order. The first was of a carved flagstone:

I was a stranger and you welcomed me.
Matthew 25

'What the bloody hell!' He attached it to the whiteboard. Apart from three, the rest seemed to be unusual shots of locations or blurred images. They were far from the normal snap; they were just parts of the floor, buildings or structures. The three that were very different, one showing bags of money, the others firearms and drugs, stood out from the others.

'Motley collection, Kasum.'

Kasum came across, moved to his side of the desk and studied the displayed photographs. She pointed to the first he had arranged on the board. 'That carved flagstone is in the garden where the phone was found.'

'Really?' He took another look. 'If that's the case it's probably the last picture taken before he stuck the phone on the statue.' The rest were time dated over a three-day period. He quickly arranged them in chronological order and stood back. Nothing jumped out at him. He turned to look at Kasum.

'Let's look on it as if it's an odyssey, Tony.'

'A what?'

'A journey, or his experience before and after being attacked. A beginning, a middle and an end although we don't really know where the end will be. We can say for now it's when the phone was discovered. He might well have been planning to take more had he not been attacked again.'

'Or on the other hand, it could be his legacy. Danny's not that bright, Kasum.' He tapped the desktop with his knuckles. 'As thick as this unless you want to know where Timbuktu is, trust me.'

'It's in Mali.'

Tony pulled a face – *I'm surrounded by smart arses.*

'You need to identify these places.' She selected one. It showed the corner of a brick wall with a number of bricks missing, forming a definite pattern. Picking it up, she studied the background. 'I think this is somewhere near the Tobacco Warehouse, either along Regent Road or Great Howard Street. You can just make out one of the stone gate's columns just there. They're unusual at that point as they're set at an angle to the walls. Many of the others along the docks are set within straight walls.' Turning, she went to a computer and searched Google Maps. On locating the place, she changed to Street View. Moving down Regent Road she occasionally paused, then she turned and looked towards Tony. 'Bingo!' she called with a broad smile.

Tony came over to the screen and stared at the close-up. The detail of the missing bricks matched perfectly. 'Bugger me!'

'If I'd known that was the reward, Tony, I'd have kept my mouth shut!'

'Sorry, Kasum, but well done! Can you work the same magic with the others?'

'I doubt it. You need to play find the locations. Think of them as a type of hieroglyph but instead of them giving words, they're offering pointers, locations around a specific place or area. You have a few to go at. This location with the missing bricks is in the process of redevelopment, but as you know, Tony, you still don't want to be wandering the side roads there after midnight!'

'What about these three?' Tony tossed them onto the desk.

'It will be a little more difficult to find a true location for the drugs, cash and weapons but they're telling part of the same story. Possibly, they're there to show that your fugitive is in deep trouble, the reason he's on the move. He needs help. Let's hope he hasn't done a runner with one or all three of these items.'

Tony put his head in his hands. 'I could never do crosswords and I was crap at finding Wally as a kid.'

'And you became a detective?' Kasum moved back to her own desk. 'Good luck! Let me know if anything else springs to mind.'

He watched her leave. She always walked with a straight posture as if she had a taut string attached to the top of her head. Wicca had informed him it was to do with her yoga practice. Maybe he should try that. He straightened his back and lifted his head. Maybe not.

* * *

Manoeuvring his wagon as close to the side of Brunswick Place as he could, Peter Firth turned off the engine. He needed a break. Although the location chosen was not ideal, it would suffice. Piles of rubbish had been fly-tipped along that edge at the point where the base of the derelict buildings bordered the road; there was no pavement. Two other wagons were parked higher up the road. Looking in his mirror, Peter laughed to see a pair of boots resting on the dashboard of the first truck. The driver was clearly asleep.

Climbing from the cab, he stretched. The place was a dump, quite literally. Beds, wire, reinforced chemical containers, a settee, a fridge freezer and a jumble of tyres of all sizes spread like a giant strand line along both sides of the road. He needed to piss. The brickwork of the building further along was blackened by fire, the charred remnants spread before it. The damaged, blackened timbers, melted plastic and burned tyres remained as testament to a probable arson attack or maybe they were the result of a carelessly discarded cigarette. Whatever it had been, it had not enhanced the appearance and the general ambience of the site. Nipping between some corrugated metal sheets blocking entry to the building, he slipped inside. He felt an immediate relief. He should not have had the third brew before leaving for work, not at his age.

The building had no roof, just the rusting, skeletal remains that criss-crossed above his head. Much of the asbestos roofing lay on the ground like huge geometric shapes. Graffiti was liberally daubed on all of the lower surfaces, but occasionally, the more intrepid artist had managed to scrawl their tag higher up near the girders. There was a steel door set within the far wall. His curiosity got the better of him. Moving to it, he pulled. It opened, but there was a reluctance as well as a protesting squeal from the rusting metal hinges. He leaned in and scanned the space; it was the smell that hit him first and a sudden movement of flies from the corner to his immediate left. His eyes, once accustomed to the gloom, saw the face, staring with empty eyes. A pigeon in the rafters fluttered and the combination of all this brought a sensory bombardment making his retreat both clumsy and swift as a shrill shriek left his lips. Backing his way through the door, he felt the immediate relief of the fresh air purge his nostrils, bringing him back to some sort of reality. For a moment he could not believe what he had just seen. Stumbling over the fragile pieces of fallen roof, he made his way to the road whilst frantically digging in his pocket for his phone. Whoever it was, he could not say if it were male or female, but they looked as if they had been there a while. He tapped 999 and responded with a quavering voice to the questions asked.

The first responder soon arrived. To his surprise there seemed to be no urgency and neither lights nor siren announced their appearance. Peter was leaning against a metal fence away from the temporary corrugated sheet door. He stood with another driver, the owner of the feet he had noticed earlier. On seeing the vehicle approach, he waved and moved up the road towards it.

'It's in there. Not pretty.' He pointed towards the rust covered corrugated sheet. 'Through the door at the far side. Bloody stinks too, considering most of the bloody roof's off.'

The paramedic popped his backpack down and ignored Peter's gesticulating arm. 'Peter Firth?'

Peter nodded.

'How are you?' He looked directly at Peter as if he were concentrating on his eyes.

'I have to admit I'm a little upset, it's not been a normal sort of day and I've been working this area some years. If I'm honest, I'm okay. I'm certainly better than the one in there, that's for sure.'

Peter pushed open the metal and pointed towards the far door. The paramedic entered. The police car arrived shortly afterwards and two officers approached Peter.

* * *

78

April and Skeeter stood looking at Tony's whiteboards as he explained the difficulty he faced. 'I also see thousands of derelict locations that would make perfect places for the lad to hole up. The problem now for Danny, he's got to move about, buy food and such like. He'll have to become nocturnal, if he's any sense.'

'If he's any sense, Tony, he'd move away, and move as far away as possible.' Skeeter grumbled. 'Whoever they are and whatever he's done, they will not forget. Retribution is coming, and from my experience, there's never a time limit.'

'Beales?' April asked.

'He's on the periphery, I'm sure, but only with Danny. If he were linked, he'd have been targeted by now and so far, he hasn't been. They also know where he lives and he can't do a runner. He's just helped Danny.'

'Find him first, Tony, I want this as a priority in the briefing tomorrow morning. Get colleagues to look at the photographs and try to start plotting where they were taken on a street plan. There's a reason they're there otherwise he'd not have left the phone.'

April moved away leaving only Skeeter. 'Give me some copies and I'll play about with them tonight. I have a friend who's particularly good with things like this, loves the more abstract puzzles. Can't promise but ...' She winked. 'What I do know, Tony, is that you need a coffee and to chew a fingernail or two, if you've any left.' Her comment did not bring the usual sarcastic response.

'I don't want to lose this one, Wicca. Don't ask me why and you're right, I'm spitting bloody feathers.' He moved to the kitchen area.

The call came in from Control reporting the discovery of another body. It was quickly followed by a call to April from DCI Mason.

'I want you there PDQ, April. According to the officers

attending, there's a possibility the fire might have been started deliberately to hide any evidence. There's also a suggestion it's another of the homeless, but as I say, that's only a suggestion. What I am sure of is that the coroner will request a post-mortem, and owing to the decomposition of the body and the fire, a Home Office pathologist will be requested.'

April felt a flutter in her stomach. In some ways it was relief that a thorough investigation would begin. This was the third body found and although the circumstances of the first and second could be explained, there was a clear chance that there was more to their deaths than was first thought.

* * *

'Dead and dead for some time. There's no fire damage to the victim. There also doesn't appear to be any fire damage to the far side of the room and certainly none within the area where the body was found.' The paramedic spoke to the officer whilst another added the police boundary tape across the road in two places, sealing quite a large area of Brunswick Place. 'Road Closed' signs were positioned at either end. Peter Firth waited in his cab. He sipped a cup of coffee, his thermos flask balanced on the dashboard. He had called his transport manager informing him of the situation.

April and Skeeter climbed from their car and immediately glanced down Dunnett Street. The police tape ran diagonally from the steel fencing to a metal security post set into the pavement on the corner of the two roads.

'Bloody hell, April, would you look at that. If Liverpool ever needed an enema, I think we've found the crevice in which it should be inserted. Have you ever seen as much crap in such a small area?'

April heard not one word, as she was already moving

towards the officer who stood before the tape. A forensic investigation vehicle was in situ. She flashed her ID.

'There are three layers to this building. The body is in the second and situated in a corner. Most of the roof is missing or at least fragmented. There is still coverage over the body and some of the collapsed roof is forming a protective wall. Maybe that's why the person selected that space if they were in fact homeless. It's closed off from the rest and far more secure.'

'Is there anything with the body?'

'Bags of rubbish and quite a few bottles and cans, all empty. From what's been said it's – sorry we don't know the gender – positioned on an old mattress. CSI are setting up lamps and cameras. The person who made the discovery is a Peter Firth. He's in his wagon down there. He seems fine. The paramedic also checked him over. According to control, we're expecting a pathologist in half an hour.'

April smiled, thanked the officer and after being signed in by the CSM she ducked below the tape. She kept to the far edge of the road manoeuvring around the detritus before slipping under the tape on the other side of the exclusion area.

She looked up towards the cab's windscreen and signalled for Peter to join her.

He immediately began to explain how he discovered the body. 'I'd only gone for a pee and it scared the shi … sorry, life out of me. Never seen a dead body before. You think you would have when you get to my age. I thought it was one of those mannequins for a second or two, but funnily enough, you soon realise that what you're looking at is real when you add the stench. To me, the skin was like wax, but that could have been the poor light. There were quite a few flies, seemed like loads but now, on reflection, there might not have been as many as I first imagined, it just seemed a lot as they moved together.'

April quickly realised he was rambling. It was either through nerves, shock or a combination of both. Once she had offered reassurance the details emerged.

Skeeter watched the pathologist arrive. She did not recognise him. He was a small bespectacled man with a balding head. His well-rehearsed routine saw him go to the boot of his estate car before methodically dressing in PPE. He checked he had all that he would require then closed the tailgate. She watched as he held the palm of his hand to his face and adjusted the powerful head torch before he approached her, his face mask dangling at his neck.

'DS Warlock. It suits you.' She pointed to his head.

He paused taking longer than a moment to look into her eyes. 'That's some contrast, if that's not being too rude on our first meeting, Detective Sergeant. Fascinating.' He bent his knees until he was face height and inspected her eyes in more detail, his head pivoting back and forth a few times. 'No relation to the churchman, I suppose, DS Warlock?'

Skeeter was already shaking her head, almost mirroring his movement. 'Different spelling, so no, he's with an "o" and I'm with an "a". Finished your inspection of me? I take it I'm still in the land of the living?'

'Yes, sorry, how very rude of me. I submitted a paper on heterochromia to a medical journal and it's been a professional fascination of mine for quite some time.'

'It was for Josef Mengele too, from what I've read. What I do know, is that these eyes scare the heebie-jeebies out of certain baddies. It's the evil eye, they tell me.'

'Mengele, yes. The least said. I can see you also keep yourself fit.' He drew his face into a sharp grin. 'No time to waste. Lead on MacDuff.' He paused and frowned. 'If you know your Shakespeare, you'd know that's inaccurate as it should be *lay on …*'

'But we're neither attacking nor are we attacking with vigor.' Skeeter turned and nodded. 'The meaning of *lay on.*'

'Very good. Not many would know that. That's why you're a detective, DS Warlock, and not plodding the beat.' He ducked under the tape and followed the strategically placed step plates leading to the now propped open corrugated metal sheeting before disappearing within.

'He's a bit of a character,' Skeeter announced to the officer who was still by the tape. They immediately checked the login notes.

'Professor Joseph Lee, no less.'

'Joseph, bloody hell I was rather close to the bone. No wonder he wanted to move on so swiftly.'

Skeeter removed her phone and typed his name into Google.

CHAPTER 11

anny Maynard sat with his knees tucked towards his chin. The sleeping bag came to just below his armpits. Light from the fragmented window entered like the missing shards, white and sharp. Watching the movement of the dust trapped within that light, it seemed to dance and fight, the movement irregular yet captivating. At that moment it was a comfort, distracting his thoughts from the predicament in which he found himself. His headache had eased. The blood had clotted and formed a crust over the recent injury. This damage had been less severe. The attackers seemed to be only kids, sixteen at most, but vile and feral. On reflection, he did not remember their faces nor their voices but their shouts and screams were still echoing in his mind. They were scousers for sure and one could sound the same as another. If he were honest, he was expecting a knife or a firearm, but again it was a bar, or was it a machete, that had made the glancing blow? He tried to remember how many there had been, maybe it was two or possibly three? It all seemed to happen so quickly.

Danny felt naked without his phone; leaving it on the statue was a gamble he had to take, both through urgency and fear. He had stripped it, apart from the numbers and the selected photographs. In his own mind, they told the story of the people and the places, but then he had little formal education so he had a limited understanding of what a useful clue might be and whether those finding them could interpret them correctly. He assumed they all had a degree of intelligence greater than his own. He knew the police had responded to his 999 call. He had seen them in the garden. The blue strobe lights had illuminated the side of the church but had they found the phone? The thought that it might still be there worried him. He would have to check once it grew dark. The thought of moving from this point of relative safety brought more than a degree of anxiety.

The sound of movement intensified all his senses. His body stiffened and he moved back gently into the recess. The next sound, a sudden crash, brought with it intense fear. 'Shit!' The word emanating from his lips was but a whisper and yet it sounded as though he had just notified the whole area of his presence.

* * *

The pathologist moved immediately to the back of his car and deposited the PPE into a small yellow surgical waste container, the final item being the second pair of nitrile gloves. He sanitised his hands. Skeeter and April walked over.

'DI April Decent and I believe you've met Skeeter.'

He raised his eyebrows. 'Skeeter, you're full of surprises. The only Skeeter I am aware of is Skeeter Davies and she sang a rather depressing song about the end of the world.'

'My grandad's favourite singer and song and I guess my mother's, too. That's where the name comes from. Is it just a bad day for you, Professor, or does being rude come as a gift from God? Besides, I would have thought the song was appropriate in your line of work and would have been amongst your desert island discs.'

April took a step back. She had quickly learned to leave well alone when Skeeter's hackles were raised.

'My sincere apologies, DS Warlock. I can only assure you I meant neither insult nor harm.'

April seized the moment to interject. 'The victim?'

'Male, white and I would say in his late fifties but I will know with greater accuracy after the autopsy. I also believe he might have been dead for four days, at most, from the degree of decomposition. Weather and temperature conditions are contributing factors to the stages of that decay. There's clear evidence of rodent damage to the face and hands which is not uncommon considering the location and the amount of rubbish that is deposited in the locality. Considering the number of empty wine and spirit bottles and cans near the body, I am, at this stage at least, making an assumption the person was home-less, or is it down and out? Anyway, whatever the new politically correct term for these folk might be, he'd been living there. There might well also be drug misuse. Will you be attending the post-mortem?'

'We will be represented. Have you any cause for concern regarding this death, Professor?'

'Suspicious circumstances? At this stage?' He did not fully commit to an answer. 'The fire to the exterior of the building might be linked – an unsuccessful attempt to destroy the body? Maybe, but then again ... Do we have a time for that? CSI are doing their due diligence and I feel their report will bring about a greater clarity and enable a more evidence-based answer to any questions we might have. But I'm ruling nothing out at this stage.' He turned directly to face April. 'I assume, Inspector, you will be SIO?'

April nodded.

'I think considering the recent history of these deaths you have enough grounds to seek further evidence. It's too easy to discard cases such as these and we know the alleged sloppy police work in the Met with drug-related cases has led to the proverbial being chucked at the fan.' He raised his eyebrows.

'If there's anything, Professor, I'm sure you'll find it.'

He turned to Skeeter. 'Please, DS Warlock, accept again my sincere apologies for my crass and insensitive comments today.' His face remained neutral as he closed the tailgate of the car.

'Bundle of fun that man. Bet his wife can't wait to greet him every night.' Skeeter turned and walked to the car.

CHAPTER 12

'That's my fucking corner, yer little twat.' The words, gruff, deep and threatening, seemed to fill the space. Danny looked across at the opening and sat upright. 'Been here every night for months and I leave it for just one and some young runt moves in as if he owns the fucking place. Well, I can tell yous one thing for nothin', you've got another think coming if ya think yous can have my bloody home.' He dropped the bag he was carrying but held onto a half empty bottle of wine before moving into one of the shards of light giving Danny a clearer view.

The man was probably in his late forties but with the length of his hair and beard, it proved difficult to judge accurately. He was lithe and relatively fit, moving without difficulty as he crossed the rubble and rubbish that formed a major part of the room's floor. One or two steel beams crossed vertically at angles adding to the obstacle course.

'There was no one here late last night. I needed a safe space. Sorry.' The last thing Danny wanted was trouble; he was in enough as it was.

'Had a visitor a few nights back, thought you might be him. I

88

gave him the bum's rush. I used to box when I was a nipper. Trained in the same gym as one of Liverpool's best, scouser like us, but he were before my time. Saw him when he came up from London and popped in – Are you from the 'Pool?' He did not give Danny time to answer. 'If not, yous can fuck right off, right now.' He wiped his nose on his sleeve before continuing. 'John Conteh's a wonderful man. Beat them in the ring and he beat the booze. He's a fucking hero. Me, I've no chance.' He tucked a bottle between his knees and started to shadow box, ducking and weaving whilst commentating on the fight. Within four of five punches he lost his balance and fell forward onto Danny's feet. The bottle disappeared from view but the resounding crash told the story. 'Don't just bloody sit there like a pile of snivellin' shite, give us a hand up.'

Wriggling from his sleeping bag Danny managed to move the boxer back into the place he had just left. Neither spoke for a moment; they both looked at each other as if weighing up just what to say.

'Thanks, lad. That was a nearly full bottle an' all. You'd have made a good cornerman. Now, what do yous have by the way of booze?'

Danny shook his head. 'I'm going out once it gets proper dark and I'll get some then.'

'You wouldn't know Conteh, would you? Yous too bloody young. The bruising you have and the cut looks like you've done a round or two.'

'It's nothing. A fall. Need to take more water with it!'

'Fucking sacrilege that, lad.' He shuffled to get more comfortable. 'Trevor, my name's Trevor, not so clever as I've often been told. Thanks for helping and keeping my space warm.' He chuckled but then thought of the lost booze. Slipping his hand into an inner pocket of his coat he brought out some change. 'Cider, a couple of bottles of the strong stuff if you'd be so kind, when you go out.' He dropped the coins onto Danny's open hand. 'That's part of my reward for begging all day and playing. If you want my advice, and I'm sure just by looking at my appearance, you don't, begging and street living's not a career you want to take up if you have the possibility of doing something else. Too many fucking weirdos, losers and nutters about.' Leaning forward he removed the rucksack and set it between his knees. 'Present company excepted, lad.'

Trevor's features were now clear. His grey and ginger beard seemed to spread to most of his face, there appeared to be no demarcation between hair, eyebrows and beard apart from a pair of round spectacles. They sat at an angle on his crooked nose. On closer inspection, Danny could see that the left lens was cracked – they seemed to magnify his eyes.

'I'm Danny. Sorry for taking your space.'

'Great minds think alike, Danny Boy. Great minds. You're welcome as you come in peace, Danny Boy.' He then started to sing, waving his arms as if conducting.

'– the pipes, the pipes are ca-al-in,
from shit 'ole to shit 'ole, along this Mersey side,
The booze has gone and all the luck is fallin',
it's you, it's you who must go and buy us all some more ...'

His singing was not only flat, but also tuneless. They both giggled as the improvisation went on. Digging in another pocket, Trevor brought out a mobile phone and then a harmonica. He played, 'Londonderry Air'. The tune was melodic, in total contrast to his singing.

'You weren't expecting that now, were you? Makes me a bob or two playing to the public. I do sea shanties they go down well.'

Danny shook his head. 'It was beautiful.' He pointed at the

phone. 'Not seen one like that for ages. My uncle had one years ago.'

'Simple, uncomplicated, not smart like me and it works so you can't ask for more than that. You hungry, Danny Boy?'

Danny nodded. 'Starving if the truth be told.'

Trevor brought out a number of foil parcels from the rucksack and placed them to the side on a rough piece of wood. 'It's not much, but you're welcome to share.'

The food, pieces of pizza, a sandwich, some cake and half of a French stick sat alongside a huge lump of cheese. It seemed like a feast. They both ate slowly and talked little, as if each mouthful had to be savoured. Danny brought out the bottle Wayne had given him from behind his sleeping bag. They shared that too.

'I'll bring some food when I come back. I shouldn't be too late.'

The spears of light had gradually faded and the room was now much darker. They both sat side by side. Trevor rolled the foil into balls and placed them on his knees. 'See the plastic paint bucket over there? It's the pisser, if you stay the night, we just don't piss anywhere, right? If you need to shit you go through there. We might be down but we're not primitive.'

'Right.' Danny screwed up his eyes as if it would help penetrate the gloom. He nodded. 'Got it.'

'Two each and we'll throw in turn. You have to get your foil ball into it. Winner gets a million pounds.' He laughed. 'That would be a fucking miracle, right Danny Boy?'

The first ball left Trevor's hand and went straight into the bucket. Danny looked at him and chuckled. 'You've done this before.'

'Maybe once or twice. Your turn.'

Danny's ball went way to the left.

'Shite shot, if you don't mind my saying so.' His arm released his second ball and that too found the target.

Danny sat up a little and took careful aim, but again he missed. 'That's a million to you, Trevor.'

'Not another one. It'll be coming out of my fucking ears at this rate!'

Within the hour Danny stood and checked he had money. It was now dark and what street lighting there was seemed to have little effect within their space. 'Is it okay for me to stay tonight? I'll still bring your cider, even if you say I can't.'

'Not had as much fun for ages. That would be great. I'm gasping for a drink so do hurry back, Danny Boy.' He started to sing once again. 'And I shall sleep in peace until you bring booze to me.' His singing had not improved but he started at the beginning singing the original lyrics as he found the blanket he had tucked safely away.

Danny stumbled in the semi-dark as the sound of the harmonica slowly diminished. Staying close to the walls and in the shadows, he enjoyed the fresh cool of the night air. He could smell the sea and he inhaled deeply. There was a freshness that seemed to flood his nostrils and clear his head. He lifted his arms in turn and sniffed each armpit; the smell was sharp and sour and in total contrast to the night air. He needed fresh clothes but more importantly, he needed a wash. He knew that a shower or a bath at the moment would be well out of reach unless Beales would help. Maybe he should save that for another day. The thought of Mrs Beales brought an upturn to the side of his mouth.

Bringing himself back to the present, he had planned to go first to the garden, then buy food and the promised drink before returning. He would, however, avoid his old haunts. His appearance would, at least, help make him more invisible to those who were charged with finding him. Within ten minutes he could see the church and the garden.

* * *

It had seemed like hours since Danny had gone and Trevor had rested his eyes on more than one occasion, but the foot treading on broken glass brought with it a sharp snap. Trevor immediately opened his eyes but remained motionless. *How long have I slept?* The question came to mind as he cautiously rubbed his eyes before dropping his glasses from the top of his head to his nose. 'Is that you, Danny Boy?' He whispered cautiously.

There was no reply only the definite sound of shoes moving over the detritus that lay haphazardly throughout the building.

'Danny Boy? No, it's not Danny Boy. I've called before. You weren't here last night. I came to find you about the same time. You're usually always here, I was told. I brought these. They're a gift. I try to help, be kind as I too have been where you are. I'll leave them here.'

The sound of the footsteps moved away. Any movement was inaudible. Trevor remained motionless for a few moments. *A gift?* The thought tumbled in his head and brought a flutter to his stomach.

The bottles were placed together. He held one to the window to catch whatever light there was and he immediately saw the honey-coloured liquid. 'This better not be passed by the management.' He had found bottles before, whisky bottles but they were filled with piss. He could, however, see they were still sealed. It took only moments for the top to be removed and his nose to hover over the bottle's neck. A smile came to his lips quickly followed by the bottle.

CHAPTER 13

April stood and looked at the results of her evening's work. The multi-coloured textured glass had been cut and placed on the cartoon, the black lined pattern that showed the stained-glass window design. The glass cutter was back in the jam jar, the cutting wheel submerged in a shallow reservoir of oil. She had enjoyed a trip to Pearson's Glass, near Kirkdale, on her return home from work. Walking within the racks of cut glass always brought a mix of pleasure and confusion. Although she had planned the window, seeing the myriad colours and textures available made her mentally reassess her design and she often came away with a greater variety of colours than she had anticipated.

Holding the mug of coffee, the end result proved that she had, on this occasion, made the correct decision. Tico yawned from the door. The child gate kept the dog out of the room away from any small splinters of glass that were often on the floor during this creative process.

'That's it for tonight, Tico.' She too yawned as she glanced at the clock on the wall hardly believing the time. 'Where does the time go when you're having fun? It's much later than I thought and we have a …' she paused not wanting to mention *walk*. 'Too early in the morning.'

Instinctively, she carelessly ran her hand over the paper cartoon that lay flat on the table, the glass having been transferred. Immediately regretted the action. The sharp sting to the tip of her finger brought a spontaneous reaction. A large globule of blood grew like a small, red balloon before bursting and running towards the palm of her hand. Bringing her thumb to her finger she pressed, hoping to extract the sliver of glass that had penetrated the skin but it only brought more blood and a deeper, stinging sensation. She could feel its presence but could not see any part of it. Taking a tissue, she wrapped it round her finger; the white turned immediately red.

'Just when you think you've cleared every last piece, made everything secure …' She spoke out loud, her frustration directed towards Tico.

The words of DCI Mason for some strange reason came immediately to mind. "Murder can be masquerading as a smokescreen." She stared at the cartoon spread over the table and lowered her gaze until her eyeline was almost level. Three more needle-sharp slithers were hiding, transparent and innocent against the white background.

"We are missing something with this case and like these they are hiding in plain sight." Removing the tissue, she brought her finger to her lips and immediately felt the embedded glass sting as the coppery taste of blood filled her mouth. "Remind me to speak with Michael tomorrow."

Tico tilted his head to one side and yawned.

Flicking off the light, she left the room and Tico followed after a full stretch.

* * *

Danny had been relieved to see the phone had gone from the upper ledge of the statue and yet the butterflies within his stomach seemed to flap with a greater urgency; the uncertainty of not knowing by whom and to where it had been taken gnawed at him. Had the police found it? Surely, after the call he had made, they must have, and, if so, did they understand the significance of what they had? His eyes constantly scanned his surroundings spending seconds scrutinising each person, their body language and, if possible, their faces. Individuals held little threat, but a group would cause him to meld into doorways or shadows. Within half an hour of arriving at the garden, he headed back out of the centre. He knew where he could buy the booze and food and for the first time he longed to be back in the ruin. The tune to 'Danny Boy' flooded his thoughts and he smiled at the idea of Trevor waiting, eager for the promised drink.

The carrier bag seemed heavy as he turned onto Fulton Street. He had a way to walk before crossing Blackstone Street. Where Fulton Street continued, the corner section comprised bushes and shrubs to the left, naturally softening the landscape and giving a false sense of urban gentility. Looking behind them at the broad, expansive dumping ground, the green façade gave only a false impression, a moment's respite. After a few steps, the full extent of neglect and decay loomed. The street's darkness was kept at bay by the orange of the few streetlights spread meagrely along its length. The height of the buildings to either side appeared to close in, the red brick now dark. All were boarded, locked or steel shuttered, as some were still viable businesses by day. They housed the heavier and dirtier elements of industry that still fed the working docks.

Moving up the road, he kept to the edge of the buildings wherever the lack of dumped rubbish allowed. He had known it when nothing was discarded, but as more and more businesses declined and the cost of waste disposal grew, the fly-tipping increased. The occasional scurrying from beneath boxes, tyres and discarded items did not bother him, he knew they could not harm him. He instinctively started to whistle, a low yet discordant melody of the tune he had heard earlier. It was more to help ease his tension than ease the anxiety that was induced by the orange-veiled darkness and the unfamiliar sounds. His eyes were now accustomed to that low light and it was then, as he negotiated a dumped settee, that he paused after seeing a figure emerge from the building to the right of the road. He knew the exact place. They had come from the door he had left a couple of hours previously. One second, he had felt he was alone and the next … fear flooded his body on realising he had company. Danny immediately froze, his whistled tune stopped too, as if suddenly trapped between closed lips. Slowly lowering his body, he tried to blend with the rubbish. He wanted to remove any possibility of his silhouette being visible. *Was it Trevor leaving?*

The figure paused to scan the road in both directions. After a few moments, smoke appeared to drift around the stranger's head and face as if trapped within the meagre light. Whoever it was had lit a cigarette before moving up the road. By observing their posture, gait and height, Danny believed the stranger to be male. He waited until they had turned out of sight before continuing. *It can't be Trevor,* he thought.

On reaching the entry to the derelict building, the smell of tobacco still lingered and he grew even more cautious, only moving inside after allowing his senses to absorb the immediate atmosphere of his surroundings. He deliberately coughed. It echoed and he waited for Trevor to call out but there was no response.

'Trevor!' Danny called. 'It's Danny.'

There was still nothing. As he paused, the silence seemed to grow treacle-thick and he could hear his own blood beat in his ears. Moving further in brought different sounds from his contact with the glass and wood that covered the floor. No matter how cautiously he trod, the noise seemed amplified. To his relief, when he negotiated the corner made up of broken brickwork, he saw Trevor leaning backwards in the corner.

'Trevor!' His voice was now louder and more agitated as the continued silence would not allow him to relax.

Approaching, he paused and crouched as he looked directly into Trevor's face. To his surprise, Trevor's spectacles were to his left. They appeared crushed, trodden onto the plank of wood on which they had earlier both sat and shared food. An empty bottle lay on his legs and another, identical, holding only about a third of its contents, was in his hand.

'Trevor!' Danny reached forward and touched his other hand, it was warm. There was no response. 'Trevor! Are you okay?' The more Danny looked at his face, the more he felt nausea grow in his stomach as the realisation that the person a foot away from him was possibly dead. His thoughts were now in turmoil and the bag he carried slipped from his hand. He did not question the presence of the bottles as guilt flushed through his whole body. *Did they follow me last night, know where I would be tonight and come to finish the job?* His thoughts grew more illogical. 'I'm sorry, Trevor, I'm sorry!' His words now were but a whisper. 'They were looking for me!'

Cautiously he stood and looked down at the body. A cold shiver ran the full length of his back and he began to shake. He could not remember the last time he had cried as tears streamed down his cheeks. His shoulders lifted and fell. Animalistic noises, grunts and snorts, seemed to be drawn uncontrollably from his nose and lips. The emptiness, confusion and fear trapped and paralysed him. Standing in the grey dark he mumbled almost inaudibly. 'This is my fault. It was meant for me, Trevor, not you. I'm sorry, so very sorry.'

Leaning forward he searched Trevor's jacket pocket and took out the phone and the harmonica. On touching the keys, the phone illuminated. There was no password or code. He held up both objects. 'Thank you, I hope you don't mind. I'll look after both and promise I'll learn to play this as beautifully as you did.'

* * *

DCI Mason entered. The chattering amongst the assembled group suddenly died as people moved to a selected chair. Mason tossed a file onto the table before him, adjusting his tie before slipping off his jacket and hanging it on the back of his chair. To the casual observer, and to the officers who had witnessed his briefings often, it seemed to be almost a ritual. He poured a half glass of water and took a sip as he scanned the room. He did a mental headcount.

'Morning.' The word was just that, no *good* to preface it, carrying little sincerity. The response was guarded.

'As you've read.' He held up a file. 'We have the forensic pathologist's report detailing the death of a Gabriel Hinds. Hinds was known to the police and not just here but in a number of neighbouring forces – petty crimes, drugs, alcohol and the occasional disturbance. He was a big man and had a reputation as a bully. Of no fixed address for some time, although he'd not been in trouble for a few months. According to the report, he died from an injection of potassium, probably as potassium chloride, as well as severe alcohol poisoning. This was not self-induced.' He tapped the folder. 'As the puncture was here.' He placed a finger to the right side of his neck.

April looked at the plaster she had applied to the end of her finger and a slight shiver ran along her arms.

'It was administered in a downward trajectory and you can see from my hand position that this would be difficult to

99

perform yourself, especially when you consider the blood alcohol content at the time. That may be the wrong way round considering what he had consumed. April?' He sat and moved the papers into a neat pile as he looked across at her.

April stood; she felt her finger throb prophetically. She nodded at the officer by the computer and on the large screen behind her, the Merseyside Police logo was replaced by an image of a building. 'As you can see, there was a significant fire at the site where Hinds's body was discovered, but the fire was contained mainly to the front of the building and to the areas directly behind the wall. There was no fire ingress to the area where the body was located, but there would have been a degree of toxic fumes. Pathology tells us he was there when the fire occurred.' She paused briefly, as a number of photographs taken at the scene appeared. 'Evidence also suggests that he was dead at that point as the PM shows there was no smoke inhalation. We know the fire was extinguished by the fire service two days before the body was discovered. The discovery was reported by a wagon driver, a Peter Firth, who rang 999 on discovery of the body. What's significant is that both firefighters and a police officer at the scene of the fire reported they'd checked the immediate buildings for any potential smoke victims and had discovered none.' She paused to let the information and the implications of that knowledge percolate through the group. 'Person or persons have cocked up! We've all read too often reports of the police not learning from, and I quote, "its calamitous litany of failures". His Majesty's Inspectorate of Constabulary and Fire Rescue Service has specifically criticised "lazy" officers and suggested police forces are "relying on luck".'

She indicated quotes with her fingers. 'The majority of these reports do not focus on this force, I'm pleased to say, and we all know to whom the report is referring, but there have clearly been errors demonstrated in this case, a serious crime, a death that is on our own doorstep. As you're aware, Hinds is the third death of someone living on the streets in less than two weeks. I don't believe anyone makes that life choice even though we've all talked to doorway sleepers in our time who tell us they wouldn't have it any other way. Many have no alternative, owing to circumstances and life choices they've made in the past, or as a result of addictions and mental health issues that have not been addressed or fully diagnosed. They fall through the many holes in today's net. However, I'm reminded of this quote by Pythagoras, and I feel it's relevant: "No man is free who cannot control himself."' She paused and looked around the room. 'Alcohol and drugs rob people of freedoms, making many reliant and compliant which often takes them to the wrong side of the law. Hinds could possibly be a revenge killing.'

'As pathology indicates he'd been dead before the fire was started, that would put it just before the chap who was discovered in Hesketh Park – Felix Spencer.' Skeeter commented as she cracked the knuckles on both hands.

'Possibly the same day. Further tests are being carried out on the two victims as they both showed higher than normal potassium content within their blood. They both had standard postmortem examinations and further imaging-based assessments were not deemed necessary, owing to the condition of the victims' organs, their lifestyles and the circumstances in which they were found. At this moment, we are treating Hinds's death as murder, and, therefore, there's a potential for a sequence of murders.' She looked at her injured finger. 'Sometimes, because things are difficult to see, they can be missed, and those careless omissions can have painful consequences." She turned to look at Mason before continuing. 'DCI Mason and I do not want it known at this early stage that we may have a potential serial killer operating in Merseyside until we have more evidence. Greater resourcing has been allocated as well as funding for further forensic investigations for both Spencer and Victoria. We've still not discovered any more about either person but with greater resources we may shed more light on both victims.'

'Why?' Kasum spoke with a degree of distress that was clearly audible. 'Why would someone kill people who were already down at heel? It certainly isn't for what they had or knew and I doubt either one of them was trading or involved in drugs, other than on a personal level.' It was almost as if she were thinking out loud.

'If only we knew, Kasum. Research any past cases where vagrancy is linked to serial murder or harm. If the motive for the killing is purely revenge, then something might become apparent. Keep it broad and go back a generation. Stick initially to the north of the country and add to the criteria potassium chloride, as that's one of the three drugs used to kill death row prisoners in America. Whoever did this will have some link to chemicals.'

'Merseyside and the Wirral are full of chemicals, biochemicals and pharmaceuticals – ICI at Runcorn, Pilkingtons, Beechams – and a shed load more. Good luck with that!' Skeeter announced.

April frowned momentarily before turning to Tony Price. 'It's not much but look at geographical location. Is there any link? Place names, buildings might hold clues. We know the bodies were not moved post death so can we assume the victims chose the place and not the killer.'

Kasum made quick notes and her demeanour seemed to change for the positive.

DCI Mason stood. 'I've organised more foot patrols and Crisis, Roof and a few other homeless charities as well as social services have been requested to further enhance the support for the homeless.' Photographs of the three victims appeared on screen. 'I want their faces on our social media platforms and in local papers. Maybe we can jog memories and find out further details of them all but, more importantly, more on the woman and the latest discovery.'

As he spoke, an officer entered and placed a typewritten note before him. He took a moment to read it before appearing to take a deep breath.

'We have another. Male by the name of Trevor. We only have a first name to date. He was found in a derelict building on Fulton Street. According to the preliminary report a man in his twenties mentioned it to a taxi driver very early this morning before running off. He told the driver he had no phone to report it; it's been confirmed and Scenes of Crime are on their way. The area has been sealed. I want Professor what's-his-name on this case. April, Skeeter, you also. I want this one tight and I want nothing leaking to the press. From this note they're already sniffing.'

* * *

James Speakman stared at the blue-and-white pieces of tape that dangled from one of the stanchions supporting the roof to the semi-derelict loading area and the other tied to a branch of the buddleia. He inhaled the nicotine from his roll up. There was always a morning calm on the canal, rarely was the day rushed. A light mist clung to the water's surface, only moving briefly, as if disturbed by waterfowl or fish. He read the white lettering that remained on the tape out loud: 'ot cross'. He chuckled briefly as he added the word 'buns'. He knew the full extent of the original wording. 'Lazy bastards couldn't be arsed untying it. To think they want coppers to have a degree before they start. They should ask for common bloody sense and nous and then …' He had seen the tape when he arrived the evening before. There was only one towpath running to the right at this point, the left bank offered security for the ribbon of industrial area. He had still taken his bike and cycled once it was dark.

He took the last drag, holding the remnants between finger and thumb, before flicking it towards the far bank as he checked the photograph on the control board. 'Three years, four months and fifteen days and so far, the genie has remained imprisoned within the glass.'

Turning the key, he pressed the start button and the diesel engine coughed, a degree of reluctance was the norm, but soon the motor started and the metronomic beat settled as grey-black smoke belched from the side of the hull. The two holding lines were set at forty-five degrees from the boat and both stakes were covered with bright orange buckets, to warn towpath travellers of their presence. Removing the first, he held the rope allowing it to slip through his fingers before moving to the back. He would roll the mooring ropes before moving off. Although the boat was scruffy, the ropes were always neat.

Back in the cockpit, he rubbed his hands on an old cloth before pushing the throttle and taking hold of the tiller. The engine note deepened and the boat began to move. For an old craft, it appeared to glide towards the bridge that ran beneath Bankhall Street, as a light mist of rain blew across the boat. He turned and looked at what appeared to be a mattress that formed part of the rubbish dumped within the ruin; it lay close to the flapping tape. A smile lit his face. Tomorrow he would be moored within the Merseyside Docks. He was on the last leg of his journey.

CHAPTER 14

D anny knew he had a long wait ahead of him. There was only one person he could trust. The light drizzle was an added inconvenience. He sat beneath the railway bridge that crossed the canal a mile from Fulton Street. He would be safe there and he would remain dry. The train rumbled over the bridge making the wall on which he leaned shiver. It was in total contrast to the canal barge that drifted towards him. The smoke from the chimney, light and grey, seemed to be dragged backwards giving the impression the boat was moving faster than it was. *To be on that and leave this place. You've been such a bloody fool, Danny Boy.* His new name seemed to come instinctively to mind along with the tune and he immediately thought again of Trevor. He was never a Daniel, recalling he was named Danny after a character in his mother's favourite book, *Danny the Champion of the World.* Some champion he had become, more a knobhead, as the saying goes. But at least she read a book whereas his dad had no interest – beer, footy, fishing, fighting and having too many odd bets were his reasons for living. When he had heard they were building a new stadium for his team on the docks, he was like a dog with two dicks. Danny stood and moved out away from the bridge and looked towards the Mersey. There it stood, the new stadium, all white arches contrasting starkly against the grey clad sky, guarded by two or three high cranes. He ducked back under and crouched, setting his back against the brickwork again.

The slow pulse of the boat's engine seemed to echo within the confines of the steel span of the bridge, nudging him back to the present. He turned to look at the approaching boat. The first thing he saw was the red bicycle folded in the front section. There was something familiar about the colour. The man at the rear was leaning on the tiller, his eyes seemed fixed on him. For some unknown reason he appeared to be a man without a care in the world. Maybe it was the cigarette trapped between his lips which hung limply, or maybe it was his general posture. He offered no expression, his head turned at the same speed at which the boat passed as if, somehow, his eyes were locked on the young man on the bank. Danny held his stare for what seemed like an age before the boatman slowly lowered his head as if in greeting, whilst his fingers removed the cigarette before flicking it towards the bank. Within a couple of minutes, he was looking the other way in the direction in which he was heading. Danny's new focus was the boat's wake colliding with the canal bank.

Pulling up his hood he stared at the chocolate brown water that quickly settled, again flat and calm. He began to reminisce again, remembering the one time his dad had brought him here, not this exact spot but close by. He had promised they would fish all day. Danny remembered how excited he had been at the prospect. He even had a rod and some maggots. His mum had put together some butties, ham, his favourite, and a large bottle of Coke. His dad had selected the spot. He remembered it was near a derelict building where thick bushes ran to and along the back of the towpath.

His father had taught him to thread the maggot onto the hook and cast. That was his one and only lesson.

'It's all about silence, patience and concentration,' his dad had instructed. 'You have to watch the float, keep your eye on it no matter what.'

Danny suddenly thought again of the boatman and looked down the canal as the vessel was just rounding a bend to the right. Soon, he would be gone forever.

He turned back to the water and focused on a floating object, a plastic bottle, seeing instead that very float all those years ago, when he caught nothing all day except the back of his dad's hand.

'I told you to concentrate, not come looking for me.' There was always anger.

'Who was she?' Immediately the second blow struck hard and fast behind the right ear. It was stinging and ringing.

'She'd lost her dog and I were helping her look for it. Do you hear?'

The ringing was so loud but his voice could still be heard.

It was best not to reply, because I had seen her before, working in the local Co-op. Some said she was a scrubber, whatever that meant, but I knew I'd never seen her cleaning the floor or the windows in the shop.

'Yer say nowt to yer Mam, do you hear?' He raised a hand – but the movement became a pull into a deep hug, the smell of perfume from his jacket unmissable. 'Let's see if we can catch some fish, son.'

I never wanted to fish again but we did.

It was always like that. If he took me out he would set me up and then leave me alone. There were a few trips to Ainsdale where he'd get a bucket, spade and little flags on sticks, then he'd disappear. 'If you make a huge castle, I'll give you a quid when I get back, but only if it's good mind. I'll go and find us some ice cream. I may be a while.' The first time was so exciting, and the castle was good – he needed fetching to come back and see it. But the woman he was with wasn't Mam and he scrambled to his feet, gave me a painful crack. That taught me. Next time, it was a quicker job to make the castle. Then, pretend to be in the SAS, belly on the sand, crawling through the dunes. He would be there for sure, pants down at his ankles, a different girl every time seeming to be half buried by him and sand. I knew what would happen if he saw me. So use stealth – don't risk a beating: crawl back to the castle and wait for the quid.

Danny looked at the underside of the steel railway bridge. The drizzle had stopped and the sun brought moving reflective patterns to the grimy undersurface.

Twelve is too young an age to watch as your mam, helped by your grandad and uncle, literally kicks your dad out. Oh he got a good kicking. The bedroom window was right above it. I watched with my sister, she was fourteen and a bitch. Still is a bitch, but at least I don't see her anymore. Her voice was angry and hard when she told me why: "Cos he's always fucking someone else's woman – you know that.'

'Why would she kick him out just for that one? He should have been kicked out for shagging all the other women I've seen him with.'

She could give a slap just like Dad's: stinging ear again. 'It's the same thing you thick twat. He's been shagging anything and everything that moves and wears a skirt.'

Some of the men Mam brought home after that were animals too. I got some good hidings. That's when I went to live with Uncle.

Danny heard a shout and the noise brought back the butterflies to his stomach and he forgot about his past. Two people, youths, one on a bike, appeared down the towpath, coming his way. Getting to his feet, he moved to the far side of the bridge and climbed the steep bank until he was on a level with the railway tracks. He slipped into the bushes and waited for them to pass hoping they had not seen him.

* * *

Skeeter parked her vehicle outside the police tape by the police car that blocked Blackstone Street next to the shrubbery before the start proper of Fulton Street. It was clear the two people standing to the right were from the press. The three-hundred-and-sixty-degree camera on a stick was a giveaway. Another car blocked Fulton Street at the junction with Boundary Street, and police tape and an officer had also been positioned at the Derby Road entrance sealing the area. There was a considerable amount of rubbish discarded on either side of Fulton Street and much of it was set against the walls of the buildings.

'Matches the mood of the sky,' Skeeter remarked to April. She kicked a pink plastic box to one side. It was then that she saw the van clearly marked with the word *Forensics* and more blue-and-white tape. There was also a greater air of efficiency as an officer moved towards them. At the same time, Skeeter recognised the professor's car. April held up her ID at arm's length. 'This is DS Warlock.' The introduction was brief.

Skeeter felt the stare, there was always a stare until she stared back and then the game stopped.

'Sorry, your eyes. Made me think of …'

'Bowie?' Skeeter finished the sentence. 'It's a cross I'm happy to carry.' She spread an exaggerated fake smile across her lips.

After signing in, April and Skeeter ducked beneath the tape and were led to the second and main cordon. 'Just a little further from the press and the public is always more comfortable.'

'Who's with the body?' Skeeter asked, her defence now lowered.

'A pathologist, he's been in there a while. Had to wait for some additional lighting for the camera.'

'I believe a PC Franzmann was first responder?' April asked as they moved closer to the police tape.

'PC Franzmann and her colleague, yes. She's there.' He pointed to the car parked next to the van in what was now no man's land. Franzmann had watched them approach and moved across. There was a brief introduction.

'He was dead but there appears to be no physical injuries visible on the body. There's also a number of alcohol containers on and near the body. To be honest with you, he appeared to be sleeping that's if you can sleep with your eyes semi-open. One thing I did notice, his spectacles were crushed and positioned near him, otherwise it just seemed like he'd passed away quietly, more than likely through self-abuse. Not ...' She did not finish the sentence but looked at April's raised finger.

'Sorry to interrupt you but that's what we have to guard against, PC Franzmann. If we go jumping to conclusions at this key stage, important evidence might be compromised. Make sure both you and your colleague give a full and detailed report. I take it you both entered the building?'

She nodded.

'We have the taxi driver coming in to give a description of the person who found the body. He may well have that individual on the CCTV they run within the car. How long has Professor Lee been in there?'

'Fifteen, maybe twenty minutes at the most. Do you want the Crime Scene Manager?' Franzmann was already moving away. She had answered her own question.

'Indeed. Thank you.' April raised an eyebrow and looked at Skeeter. 'Maybe her first fatality. It affects people in different ways.'

The CSM was dressed in PPE as he approached.

'The secured route through to the body is a mass of detritus, broken brickwork, roof beams and glass before you even look at what's been dumped in there. The initial cordon attracted quite a bit of attention at first. The man found is known locally. Let's say he's a regular and quite liked from the reports we've received. This is his spot most nights unless he can't get back.'

He held an imaginary bottle to his lips. 'Maybe drugs too, but he's never a problem according to those who work in the area and have met him. Plays a harmonica around the Pierhead or close to the main shopping centre. The chap over there heard him playing last night when he was locking up his premises.'

April turned to look at the building.

'Trevor was in here?'

'The details of the witness are here. He works across there.' He continued to point in the direction of a doorway on the opposite side of the street.

Skeeter looked at the electronic tablet he held. 'I'll have a word, thanks.' She nodded to the CSM and moved towards the building set a little further down the street, pausing at the steel door. The shutter was now raised and she pressed the intercom.

The CSM continued. 'We now have images of the victim and his surroundings.'

Handing April the iPad, he moved away slightly allowing her more personal space.

The first photograph showed Trevor propped against the wall his head to one side. She slowly flicked through the images trying to get a perspective of the location and the body's position within the room. The clarity was not ideal as the artificial lighting cast shadows and made discerning scale and perspective difficult.

'You'll shortly see a close up of the right side of the neck, DI Decent.' The voice had changed.

The sudden interruption startled April but she instantly recognised the voice. 'Professor.'

It was a déjà vu moment. The man before her was clothed in PPE, his mask was held at his throat and the headtorch shone directly into her face.

'Your light is on, Professor.' She scrolled through flicking the screen with her finger.

He removed the torch and looked for the switch. 'There. Go back one. You see. It's faint owing to the hair and dirt on the skin but it's definitely a puncture wound. Right side, as in the previous case. It's near the sternocleidomastoid and I'm assuming it was injected into the retromandibular vein; again, a downward trajectory. From what I can make out there appears to be no swelling suggesting it was not clumsily injected into the muscle or surrounding tissue which might prove our man Trevor was totally out of it – in an alcoholic stupor or worse allowing our killer to locate the selected site with little difficulty. If again potassium chloride was injected, the normal effect on entering the bloodstream would be very severe for the recipient. It would signal to every muscle to contract. However, if the person is in a semicomatose or comatose state through the consumption of a huge amount of strong alcohol, that would be nullified to a greater degree. May I?' He pointed to his PPE.

'Please, I hate wearing it myself.' April continued to look through the photographs.

'One never feels properly dressed whilst wearing that. Is DS Warlock not with you?'

April nodded and then looked away from the screen. 'Interviewing a witness who heard Trevor playing his harmonica last night, suggesting, unlike the previous victim, he hasn't been dead that long.'

'Seven hours at most, is my professional assessment.'

'CSI will be spending quite some time at this scene. With what's gone on there's a need to get this right.'

The professor nodded to the CSM and thanked him, ducked beneath the tape and began to move to his car. 'I take it DS Warlock will be joining me for the post-mortem?'

'I'm sure she wouldn't miss it for the world.'

* * *

April waited in the car. There was now an urgency to find as much forensic evidence as possible. She peered through the windscreen to see if any of the buildings had any CCTV cameras attached, but then why would they? They would not last too long here. A request had been made for any footage in the areas where the bodies had been located and those would be enhanced where necessary and checked.

Skeeter opened the driver's door. 'Fascinating. What an articulate and charming individual. Looking where he works, you'd think he'd be as rough as a docker's arse. All can be deceptive – book and cover, comes to mind. He told me he used to hear him play his harmonica regularly when he was locking up late and often dropped him a few quid when he saw him about town. He also brings food when his wife had cooked more than they need. He charged his phone for him as well. He'd often ring the bell and request a recharge. He found Trevor harmless and polite, so why would someone kill him? Here's the best part. Our man did hear him playing last night.' She paused. 'The tune was, "The Londonderry Air".' She turned and looked at April.

'Anything else?' There was little in the way of response.

Skeeter could see her colleague's thoughts were elsewhere. She started to sing: 'Oh, Danny Boy, the pipes, the pipes are calling.' She paused as the expression on April's face changed, her car door was thrown open and she jogged up to the second police cordon waving at the CSM.

'Have you seen a mobile phone or a harmonica on or near the body?' April was breathing more heavily than she expected.

'Five minutes.' The CSM moved towards the entrance and spoke with one of the forensic team. They disappeared. April checked her watch, her beathing calmed. Then, 'Nothing, he had a few quid in change, and two five pound notes but neither of those objects. I've made a note and will contact you if they turn up. You've seen the state of the place. We'd been looking for the phone and the harmonica since hearing about them from the witness.'

April jogged back to the car. 'No phone and no harmonica, but cash.'

She frowned as Skeeter started singing: '... the pipes, the pipes are calling ... you!' Skeeter looked and grinned at her colleague. 'Was Danny Maynard there last night and was Trevor serenading?'

April pulled a face that displayed she could see the possibility. 'We have his DNA and we can certainly check if he's been there.' She would set the ball rolling on her return to the office.

CHAPTER 15

Skeeter waited by the gate to her cottage. The traffic was light and the smell from the restaurant opposite made her feel hungry. It was seven o'clock and the sun had another hour before it would dip, leaving the evening unusually warm and balmy. She had felt similarly about a couple of men in her past, but this time, Steve seemed different. She felt special when she was with him and excited when they were due to meet. If she could stop those emotions she would and although she had tried to cast the thoughts of him aside, they crept back with an unnerving ease. She would run with it.

'You waiting for the late posty or that fine young man of yours, young Skeeter?'

The smell of tobacco drifting over the hedge was the only signal she needed. 'The posty, Tom.' She turned and looked down at his grinning face.

'Pull the other it's got bells on. It's that fella. I can see it in your eyes.' He looked up towards the gate which was set well above the path. 'Even from here there's a twinkle.'

'In both or just …' She paused as a voice from Tom's doorway was clear and direct.

'If he's causing you any grief, lass, just let me know. He's just a nosy old so-and-so.' Tom's wife waved. 'Have fun. Your brew's by your chair, Peeping Tom, so don't let it get cold. And don't leave that fag end in the garden! Do you hear?'

Tom took a long and final drag and bobbed down to stub it out on the stone path. 'I hope Steve behaves like me. Then you'll be happy ever after and he'll be henpecked and shackled.' He chuckled. 'Have a lovely night. I love the bones of her really.' He raised a hand and went back in.

Owing to the limited daylight remaining, Steve drove them to the Beacon at Ashurst.

Skeeter looked at the vast spread of land before them. 'It's like we're on one of your drones. In each and every direction we can see for miles.'

Before them was Skelmersdale and then the Lancashire Plain. Further into the distance, the docks at Liverpool and then the Welsh Mountains were clear despite the haze brought by the setting sun. Even the Irish Sea shone with a hint of gold.

'Ashurst Beacon is a high point. You can be seen for miles. Did some of my early drone training up here with lads from Lancashire and Greater Manchester. Keeping an eye on the drone at first was critical. Part of the rules of flight. How's your local geography, Skeeter? Tell me what you can identify?' He slipped an arm around her shoulders and she let her head nestle against his chest.

She pointed. 'The mushroom water tower at Ormskirk, we'll forget Merseyside for the time being. St Helens and the chimneys of Pilkington's Cowley Hill factory.'

'And the one behind us, to the east?'

Skeeter laughed. 'Heinz, once the largest food factory in northern Europe right on our doorstep. Might still be for all I know.'

They sat without speaking and just admired the myriad

clouds now tinged and edged in yellows, oranges and red. The sky was almost turquoise.

'We have a strange case at the moment, and April and Mason believe we may have a potential serial killer. There's also a possible link with a young no-mark who's gone missing. The first two deaths seemed clearly self-induced, alcohol mainly, although the first death was thought to be suicide – it wasn't, ruled out at autopsy. Tracking their past has not been easy. Once they reach a certain point in life, let's say they end up at the nadir of their social standing within society, they seem to vanish, especially if there's no DNA held. It was only with the penultimate death that the alarm bells began to sound.'

'According to police regs, suspicion should be considered in all death-related cases until proved differently.' Steve responded as if quoting from a police manual. 'That's why they link a DS at least to each one.' He shuffled on the blanket.

'A bollocking was truly given, subtle it might have been but a bollocking is what it was. It was made clear and although fingers were not directed at anyone individually, they were pointed. Sloppy police and firefighters.'

'Who's the no-mark, and what's the link?'

'Danny Maynard. Not long out from a short spell in prison. In his twenties. Since his release, he's received a couple of good hidings. The information came from a long-term neighbour, but after the second beating, he called 999 before leaving his phone for us to find. He then disappeared, although we know he's still out and about.'

Steve frowned. 'How would he know you'd find it or was it really left for someone else?'

'We found it and we believe he intended it for us. It contained numbers, not many, and all no longer connected, but he also left a collection of photographs. There's a possibility he's directing us to who, where and why but we can only guess at

117

present – some kind of odyssey someone suggested!' She turned and looked at him and raised her shoulders. 'One photo is of a damaged wall near the Tobacco Warehouse. One is a carved flagstone in the garden next to the Parish Church, that's where the phone was left on the steps of the Blitz Memorial. Maybe that's also a clue as it depicts a woman trying to bring a child to safety whilst the lad has his arm in the air. There are others but they don't have a relevance at present.'

'Really? You said he was a no-mark. The no-marks I know don't know whether it's Easter or Pentecost, let alone leave subtle clues to help the police investigate.'

'Never underestimate a desperate man.' Skeeter moved away slightly so she could look him in the eye.

'So, what's the connection with the deaths of the less fortunate?' Steve asked.

'The latest death is a guy called Trevor. He was heard playing "Londonderry Air" on his harmonica in the place he slept and on the evening of the night he died. That's the tune to—'

'"Danny Boy". Go on.'

'Brighter than you look. One of the photographs showed a van, a knackered white van. We found it at the end of Fulton Street, one of the buildings there is where Trevor was found. We now know the victims died from a huge intake of alcohol, and toxicology identified unusually high concentrations of potassium in their systems. We also know that two of the victims had puncture marks to the neck.' She placed her finger on his neck at the location. 'Get them blotto and then come back for the denouement when they can't resist.'

'So, if I follow your thinking, you believe Danny may be the killer?'

'Not sure. We need to know if he'd been there, and we'll know once forensics have done their stuff. I need a beer.'

'We can sort that but before we do, tell me why someone

would kill four down-and-outs in the way you describe?' He stood and pulled her to her feet.

'We haven't a clue. Why does any killer kill?'

'Revenge, the power of controlling life and death, the morbid fear of rejection.'

'Availability, vulnerability and desirability.'

'Correct and many more, sometimes for no reason at all. I've done the checking. If we know the victim's past, we should be able to tie things together and eliminate others. Remind me to show you the photographs. You might have some ideas.'

'Now that beer, Skeeter.'

'Providing there's no further shop talk,' Skeeter instructed as she took the blanket.

'I'll buy.'

'Music to my cauliflower ear!' She linked his arm and they moved towards the car.

* * *

Danny Maynard sat crouched in the corner of Beales's shed, the only one devoid of domestic and gardening equipment. The diffused light from the outside lamp, positioned on the corner of the house, filtered through an old, yellowing net curtain strung across the window on what appeared to be string, allowing it to sag in the centre. It seemed to attract spiders and webs, adding to the privacy it provided. He had been here so many times; it was almost like home. It was dry, warm and safe.

He tumbled the harmonica in his hands, the chrome glistening before he brought it to his lips. Blowing gently, the sound was louder than he had anticipated. He stopped blowing. He knew the forensic people would find his sleeping bag; they would find his DNA; it would be everywhere. Would they believe he had killed Trevor? Would they think he was now a murderer as well as a dealer and all-round no-mark? He closed his eyes and thought of school.

The map, the bloody map. How often had the kids told him, dared him to do things and like a fool he complied. It was a laugh, at the time, unless you were the teacher. They were never caught, but he was. 'Danny's not a grass,' they'd say and pat him on the back at home time. Danny was good for mischief, game for a laugh. Why could I never say no?

The noise by the shed door brought him back to his senses. It opened to reveal the silhouette of Mrs Beales. 'I saw you sneak in, Danny. Thought you'd be hungry. There's some butties and a brew. I'll not tell Wayne and you don't either. He's snoring on the settee. When he goes to work, you can pop in. You know just where I'll be. Those bruises still look sore. My little gladiator.'

The door closed. Danny could immediately smell the strong, sweet tea and that was more important than the thought of what was expected of him later. He lifted the slice from the top of the sandwich, it was ham. She knew he liked ham. He held it before taking a large bite, remembering the day she had seduced him. It was all so strange, so wrong but yet exciting. He even remembered her words – 'Me and Wayne haven't got you an eighteenth pressie, but I thought as he's out you might like …' – It was the first time. It became regular and she would slip him a few quid afterwards. 'Never look a gift horse in the mouth,' she often said as she beckoned him in when the coast was clear. She also helped hide drugs and on one occasion a handgun, not that she was aware of it. He made up all sorts of stories and she seemed to just accept them without question. What was strange, Wayne never knew or if he did, he said nothing. Maybe it was one job fewer for him to do!

He sipped his tea and leaned back against the shed wall. The one consolation was he would get a shower, shave and collect some of his clean clothes from his uncle's. Hopefully he would then smell and feel human once again. He also had a small stash of drugs hidden away and he would enjoy indulging when the time was right and he could relax.

* * *

Michael Peet sat before a whiteboard containing the thirteen photographs. He had arranged them in the shape beginning with the three showing actual objects. To the right were those already identified and to the left those that continued to present an enigma.

He let his hand lift another sandwich from the plastic container he nursed on his knee; he was working through his lunch even though the clock showed just after midnight. He read the lettering – *I was a stranger and you welcomed me.* 'Matthew 25.' He muttered to himself, took a pen and jotted down the name on a notepad. His eyes glanced at each of the unidentified images and stopped at one showing what appeared to be part of a metal structure. Putting down the sandwich container, he moved to the computer and searched for images of a sculpture he had often seen on Shore Road, Southport. He typed in a broad description identifying the road, sculptures and Southport. Amazingly, a considerable number were found from the one-legged diver, a shoal of metal fish on poles, an upside-down cyclist but then the one he had been trying to locate.

Downloading the image, he magnified the area that most resembled the close-up image they had. 'Yes, there it is, in all its glory. You, beauty!' He had acquired the habit of talking to himself when working alone, on most occasions he had no idea he was doing it. The matching part was an element of the structure that resembled the Chrysler Building. He focused on the aircraft, a skeletal representation showing an Electra aircraft that flew from Southport to America, hence the sculpture including a representation of waves and two skyscrapers. He immediately cross-referenced that with the Blitz memorial in the church gardens. Both included aircraft. 'Is it pure coincidence? Am I trying too hard to find connections?'

He finished the last sandwich, unwrapped a Tunnock's Caramel Wafer and dangled it out of his mouth like a large cigar. He logged onto the police database, typing only the name 'Matthew' followed by the word 'Merseyside' and a narrow date-of-birth window. He was surprised that so few results came up. He checked the last names linked, looking for one in particular: Merrill. It was a stab in the dark. On the third page between Mansell and Muldoon, was a Matthew Merrill. Digging a little further, he discovered Merrill would now be twenty-nine. He had, according to the attached record, a very chequered past – drugs, theft with intimidation and violence – but nothing had been reported within the last two years. The chocolate began to melt, and he took a bite of the biscuit whilst leaning back in the chair. His extracurricular lunchtime work had produced some results as well as a smile.

He glanced at the clock on the wall, he had five more minutes of his own time. He scrolled further before printing the results. Matthew Merrill, it seemed, was no longer resident in Merseyside. His last known address was a short-term rental in Telford after completing an eight-month prison spell. He finished the biscuit and wiped his mouth on the back of his hand.

'Where are you now, Matthew, is the million-dollar question.' Leaning towards the printer he collected the four sheets of paper.

* * *

Even though it was very late, Skeeter sat at the kitchen table with the mystery photographs spread before her. Steve had picked them up one at a time.

'Who has welcomed whom?' he asked whilst reading the paving stone inscription before stifling a yawn.

'The whom is Danny, the who could be anyone, but they are in here I know it.'

'Looking at the money on this photograph I'd say there's possibly two hundred grand, maybe more. I've never seen what that amount would look like so let's give or take the odd thousand. If your Danny's gone off with that then it's not going to take them long to find him. They'll not assassinate him either as they want to know where he's stashed the money. These two attacks may well have been rough attempts at kidnap.'

'Rough attempts?' Skeeter turned to look at him. 'If those were attempts, we're dealing with lower-league criminals here, kids being paid. Had it been premiership criminals, he'd have just disappeared, talked and vanished without trace before he'd have the time to play this silly bloody game.'

'Are the firearms fake or real?' Steve asked.

'No way of knowing from this.' She tossed the photograph onto the table. 'I know one thing. It's bedtime and your home time. I'd invite you to stay, but …'

Steve frowned, stood and grabbed his jacket but then paused as he leaned over to shuffle the photographs with some urgency. He picked up one that contained just a series of hatched black-and-white lines. 'Can I take this?'

Skeeter nodded. 'You know where it is?'

'It's a hunch, that's all.' He raised an eyebrow. 'I'll let you know if I'm right. It's been fun. Ring me. Tomorrow?'

'Tumble Tots tomorrow. I'm at the wrestling club. Come if you want!'

'Thanks, I'm washing my hair.'

CHAPTER 16

The sound of a car starting woke Danny. The shed was in full darkness until the moving lights from the reversing vehicle penetrated the net curtains. It was Wayne on his way to work. He waited until the engine noise had faded. Leaning forward, he rubbed his legs to help generate blood flow before standing. His body seemed to ache but the idea of a shower, some hot food and whatever else Mrs Beales had in mind seemed to help alleviate his immediate worries. Opening the door, he moved towards the kitchen window. The room was still dark but the Venetian blinds were not fully closed, allowing him to focus on the microwave clock; it was only 2.17. He checked again, after rubbing his eyes. *Why has he gone so early?* The confused thought did not help. *Had he been called in, was there a problem with the production line, staff absence?* Looking up, he saw that the bedroom was still in darkness. He tried the back door but it was locked. He moved back to the shed. He needed to check something.

The small headtorch was where it always was, hanging from a hook above the workbench. He needed the red filtered light – it would protect his night vision and not throw too much light outside. The room took on a low, warm, red glow. He slipped it onto his head before lying flat. Danny leaned under the work bench slowly moving a pair of boots to one side before stretching as far as possible to retrieve a long piece of round plastic waste pipe from the very back. The end was covered with thick canvas held in place by a number of elastic bands. He removed it and placed it by his knees before slipping his hand in one end. He felt the cold of a polythene bag. He extracted the first wedge of bank notes, they too were wrapped in an elastic band and fitted the diameter of the pipe perfectly. Inside there were more, but he only needed to extract the one packet.

After careful consideration, he opened the bag. He counted two hundred twenty pound notes onto the floor before putting the rest back as he had found them, securely replacing the temporary lid. Taking these would mean there would be no turning back, he had no way to repay the money. The act was done and whether what had been taken was in full or only part of their money would make little difference to them. He folded the notes and put them in his pocket before concentrating on the other end of the tube. That too was sealed in a similar way. Inside, the brown protective paper wrap was warm to the touch and in direct contrast to the cash he had withdrawn. He removed it and unwrapped the object from the paper – the gun fit his grip perfectly. Holding the weapon took him back to when he was once a Nogzy soldier, a defiant ten-year old gang member who thought he was the bee's knees and hard as nails; a time when he was the ferret, the carrier and courier, too young to prosecute if caught. It was now just that, a memory, an experience that had brought both pleasure and fear in equal measure, but one he had thrived on. However, that soon changed when Matthew came on the scene just before the 'soldiers' were busted. It was as if Matthew had a sixth sense and he offered strong guidance, even though their age difference was minimal.

He would make them rich, untouchable and they seemed to be just that, untouchable, always ahead of the game, until the moment he was caught. He remembered the day clearly, but more importantly, he remembered Matthew's defiance and his words, 'I'll be back like the mythical bird, Danny, you just watch.' Danny thought he meant the Liver bird but was later told it was another one.

Danny believed meeting again was by chance but that was not the case. What he did know, it was good to be back working for him, with him – he was a ferret again, pushing, trading and earning whilst feeling protected and part of a family. Even though Matthew had changed his name, he was still Matthew to Danny. This was his gun, Matthew's gun. He wanted to take it but thought better of it, quickly replacing the oilpaper around the gun and returning it within the pipe. Immediately the red glow seemed to match the sudden change of mood that flushed through him, it was a mixture of anger and frustration, each emotion vying for dominance. He had been a fool at times and he acknowledged it in moments of clarity. He rolled the tube back beneath the bench as tears filled his eyes. *You've been a fucking fool.* His thoughts tumbled, stoking his turmoil, as Wayne's words came immediately to mind: 'You'll be a clown amongst clowns in the circus of fools!'

Returning it all now would be too late. He knew the idea to get rid of Matthew was the only way forward. When he thought it through, it made sense. No one else knew it was there. The police knew him as Matthew Merrill and without shouting it from the rooftops, without being seen to be a grass, they could find him if they could interpret the clues. If they found him there would be more than enough evidence to put him away for a long time.

The early dawn light penetrated the net curtains as he heard the shed door latch open.

'I've run you a bath, Danny, there's a brew on the table and some toast. I bet you're starving.'

Danny closed his eyes briefly. Suddenly the world, his world, had become a better place.

* * *

After reading Michael's overnight epistle, April picked up the drumsticks from the corner of her desk and tapped out a brief rhythm. Her hand movements were delicate and the touch of the tips light and precise on the surfaces they struck. The action helped relax her shoulders and gave her a moment to let his message sink in. The phone rang. To her surprise it was Michael Peet.

'Think of the devil.' The surprise in her voice still evident.

'Whatever happened to good morning, DI Decent?'

'Sorry, yes, good morning. I've just finished reading your note.'

'Forgiven. I hoped I'd catch you. I forgot to add something I'd been working on during my break.' He continued to describe further the finer details before mentioning Matthew Merrill. 'It's probably one of my long shots but I'm convinced it's positively inspirational. The last trace we had for him was in Telford. Nothing from there. Seems to have blended like the down-and-outs who have been causing you a headache. I checked across the notes too. Your first chap, Felix Spencer, came from that neck of the woods but again, that's likely to be pure coincidence. I see Matthew Merrill and Danny Maynard pretty much match according to their police history. Age difference is not great. I can't link their early years, but then there are quite a few disparate gangs and groups spread throughout the city. Both Matthew and Danny have been inside for similar misdemeanours, as you know. The one explanation for losing

Matthew that I keep coming back to is a name change, no longer is he Matthew Merrill but ... I feel sure we'll crack it when we know the location of the other photographs. One is bugging me, the blurred blue-and-white one, I just can't get my head around it but I will if it's the last thing I do!'

'I'm sure, but we have to trust your first long shot, and ...' April did not sound convinced but she knew Michael's track record and he was rarely wrong.

Michael agreed, but there was nothing else at this stage. He explained his reasoning and the more he said the more April could follow his logic. The call ended.

Moving through to the whiteboard containing the photographs taken from Danny's phone, she checked them against the images Michael had left. They believed they had another match. She could also see how he had deciphered the link between the obscure photograph, the statue and the name Merrill, but she could also see that it would be easy to fall into the trap of wanting to see, and therefore creating, their own scenario. The difficulty in understanding the logic was putting Danny Maynard into that same complex thought process. If he were without real intelligence, as Tony had suggested, how could he contrive subtle and quite complex clues such as these? There was not only a logic to it but a lateral and abstract thought process. There was also no guarantee someone would perceive it in the same way.

Skeeter entered holding a mug of coffee.

'Just the person I need as a sounding board.'

Skeeter lodged herself onto a desk and allowed her legs to swing. 'All ears, fire away.'

April explained the clue and the lead they believed had come from it. There was a long pause after April had finished.

'Danny Maynard's no fool. He's avoided us for quite some time and yes, I feel he could create a clever series of clues. Some people have that way. They can do those cryptic crosswords, program computers, but they often have other weaknesses within their personality. Whether he's confident they will be interpreted and acted upon is anyone's guess. What's the purpose? What's his end game?'

'If we knew that we'd be halfway to understanding. Put the word out on the dark grapevine about Matthew Merrill and see if anything comes in. Someone might be prepared to say something for a consideration. There's usually someone whose desperate enough. We also need to locate the other places or objects on these photographs.'

Skeeter's mobile vibrated but did not ring. It was Steve.

'The photograph I took yesterday, I think I'm right. If you can Street View Foley Street and look at a gable, look at the bottom corner. I think you'll find a match. I'll leave you to draw your own conclusions. It's also close to the area of the three latest deaths. Must fly.'

'Literally I take it!' Her words fell on deaf ears.

April glanced at her; anticipation clearly etched on her face.

'Steve. He had a hunch last night about one of the photos, might be more ...' She jumped from the desk and moved to the computer and followed his guidance. April joined her. She zoomed in on the black-and-white mural of the Beatles, painted on the gable end of a pub, focusing on John Lennon's collar. April went to the whiteboard and removed the similar photograph. It was a match. 'That's painted on the side of The Phoenix Hotel!'

As the words came to her lips, both turned to look at each other.

'Who has risen from the ashes?'

'A pound to a penny we're looking for one Matthew Merrill. His new pseudonym will be hidden in the photographs we have yet to decipher.'

Using the Merseyside street map, they plotted the new location to that of the other places identified from the photographs, whilst also adding the locations of the deceased. Also included were Danny's last known residence, the uncle's house and the location of Beales's place of work. It was beginning to form quite a tight circle.

'It resembles a noose.' Skeeter drew it with her finger connecting the pointers. 'The one that seems out of character is the death in the park.'

* * *

Mrs Beales was snoring loudly when Danny slipped from her bed. Somehow, she did not seem as pretty with her mouth agape and for the first time he could see the sagging skin around her eyes in the clear light of the morning. *Any port in a storm*, came immediately to his mind, followed by the names of a string of harbours he could visualise on the world map he carried imprinted in his head. He could still smell her on his skin as he slipped into the shower. He dressed in his old clothes knowing it would be only for a brief time before leaving, taking the forty pounds she had left on the kitchen table for him; his 'gigolo' money she called it. Within ten minutes he had changed into fresh clothes at his uncle's house, packed some others in a rucksack and called a taxi. Today, he was coming from the dark, taking a step into the light, a move he needed to take. If the police thought he was responsible for Trevor's death, the task of hiding would prove to be far more difficult. He needed time, time for them to work out the message he had sent; that was now his only lifeline.

The idea of sleeping rough again was out of the question. He had crossed a line by taking the money and he would sink or swim by that decision. He needed time to think, time to develop a more secure strategy.

The canal towpath always seemed the safest way to move towards the city, having many possible exit routes should they be needed. Fortunately, the day had remained fine apart from the slight breeze that seemed to channel its way along the waterway. He grew more positive the closer he came to his planned destination.

Stanley Lock Flight was empty of both people and canal craft. The flight comprised a series of four locks that brought boats down from the Leeds and Liverpool Canal to the water level within Stanley Dock. The railway and the road ran over a section at this point offering graffiti artists carte blanche to doodle to their heart's content on the many walls. From what Danny could see, they had taken full advantage of the opportunity.

Crossing the road, he entered the upper gate of the Titanic Hotel and within just a few steps he had entered a different world, a refined world trapped within four secure walls. The cobbled courtyard stretched towards the lower road and the hotel, once a huge warehouse, was now a jewel in the dock area's developing crown. He stood momentarily watching people coming and going, either to the gym or into the hotel; real people living secure and what looked like uncomplicated lives. More than anything he wanted to be part of that world and leave the clown world behind. If his plan worked, he could succeed.

The reception area was equally as grand. He had heard about it but he had never summoned the courage to enter. Models of the huge four-funnelled White Star Line vessel were displayed and he could not resist walking over to look at one. For a moment, he was a child again. The industrial architecture linked with the modern design took his breath away. He moved to the bar, ordered a beer and found an empty table. The beer was brought out quickly and being called 'sir' made him feel special. He paid. This area was equally as impressive. It made him shiver, tingle with what could only be described as pure excitement.

He stared across the expanse of water as a ripple broke and danced across the dock's dark surface. It drew his eyes to the Tobacco Warehouse opposite. Major work was being carried out to transform it into beautiful and expensive apartments. It had not always been like that. Then the area away from the river still resembled the derelict and run-down building to his left, the very place he had last met up with Matthew, the day the untouchable was arrested. A shipment had arrived and had iron-ically been placed in the warehouse prior to distribution. It was one of the largest they had dealt with. He even remembered his exact words as he stared each of his *ferrets* in the eye, one after the other. Matthew spoke to them quietly, he recalled. 'If we carry on like this, I'll be buying a place in here, you mark my bloody words and you ferrets will not be far behind.' He chuckled at the memory. Within the hour, Matthew was on the way to being banged up for a couple of years, by which time some of the apartments would be finished and sold. And yet, as he sipped his beer, now he was back, he would not be surprised if Matthew had moved in.

Just below him were some wooden pontoons, parallel and ordered like the rest of the hotel. Two canal narrowboats were moored, their paintwork shone as one owner was polishing the brass porthole window frames; they were obviously well loved.

CHAPTER 17

Finishing the beer, Danny moved inside, and after a great deal of deliberation, he approached reception. The receptionist welcomed him with a smile, and he felt his shoulders relax.

'Hi, I'd like to book a room for two, maybe three nights.'

She went through the options and he rejected the cheapest one. She slid the registration form across the desk along with a pen. 'Do you have a car parked?'

'No, I don't live far away. I have work going on in the house and you know what that can be like,' he lied.

'Tell me about it.' Her reply was sincere. She added his address to the computer. 'I'll need to swipe your card. Nothing will be deducted until check out.'

Danny laughed, more out of embarrassment but he thought quickly. 'That's why I'm here, that's why the work at home. Fire, destroyed the kitchen and my wallet was on the kitchen table.' He raised his eyebrows. 'But worse things happen at sea I guess.' He pointed to the *Titanic* model.

She chuckled. 'Sorry about the fire. Our life is in our phones and our cards.'

'My phone too. Fortunately, I have an understanding bank so I have cash. If that's a problem I ...'

'We normally only take cards but let me check with my manager. I'll be a few minutes.' She left and disappeared behind the screen. She was smiling on her return. 'We can always make exceptions when guests have had some bad luck.'

'I'll pay for the room now and any extras at the time I order.' He sounded confident and began to enjoy the experience. He was neither planning to cheat, nor steal and the feeling gave him a strange sense of achievement. In an amusing way, he felt adult. He completed his registration under his uncle's name and address. The name, Stan Nellist, really did not suit him, but it was all he had.

Within minutes he was directed to his room. It was huge, clean and civilised. A quick look round brought more tears, tears of pure joy. 'This is you, Danny, not living in shit holes. You were promised this life, you took the risks so enjoy every minute.' He talked to no one but himself. For a few days he knew he would feel human again.

* * *

Arcanum was steered beneath the black pipe that traversed the canal at the entry point to the Stanley Flight. James Speakman checked his watch, it was 14.10. He had booked the passage using a false name, a name he'd used since buying the boat, and a name he was known by to officials on the canal. He had been delayed nearly twenty-four hours owing to a booking error for Salthouse Dock, the last mooring before leaving Liverpool. Stanley Dock would be a temporary mooring until the following afternoon, owing to the rulings set for the Liverpool Canal Link. Inward to Stanley Dock was allowed from 13.00 until 16.00, except Tuesdays. He knew, however, there could always be a degree of flexibility. Leaving traffic were allocated the morning. At other times, the locks were padlocked. The lock keepers were already there to aid his passage. All was well with the world.

James removed the chimney after checking its attached chain as a precautionary measure, as the final road bridge over the very bottom of the flight had a minimal air draught of 2.6 metres. Within the hour he would be moored and enjoying a well-deserved coffee and some food.

Arcanum was clearly the poor relation as it moored between the two narrowboats already in position. The red folding cycle and the plethora of other items strapped and tied gave it the appearance of a pauper amongst princes. Yet it caused James no embarrassment. The boat was his home, his business and it carried his life at a pace that he directed.

Looking at the control panel, he brought a finger to the face that stared back, a face that always smiled no matter what the circumstance or the weather.

'Nearly another round trip completed,' he said but as always there could be no response.

* * *

Danny looked from his room window. There were now three boats. He frowned as he focused on the new addition. He had seen it before, recognising the red folding bike and the vessel's general untidy condition. He leaned on the windowsill in the hope of seeing the boatman but he was nowhere in sight. Grabbing his jacket, he left the room, his curiosity piqued for no other reason than that he had little else to do.

Ordering a beer and grabbing a menu, he headed outside. More tables were occupied as the sun now bathed the area in warmth, but he found one nearer to the metal bascule bridge and away from the boats. He read the names, *Mischief*, *The Wanderer* and *Arcanum*. He was unfamiliar with the term; the others made sense.

The waitress arrived with his beer, a small bowl of crisps and an electronic tablet on which to take his order. For some reason he felt as though he were an imposter, out of his depth and soon to be revealed as a cuckoo in their nest.

'Have you decided on food?' The few words helped his nerves subside as he picked up the menu. He looked for ham.

'A ham and cheese toastie with fries, please.'

'That's my favourite,' she responded quickly.

Danny sensed she was flirting but could not be sure. 'The boat there, *Arcanum*, I think it said, do you know what the word means?'

The waitress looked at the direction in which he was pointing. 'No, sorry. It's so scruffy it's cute.'

Danny looked down at his unpolished shoes. Maybe she thought the same about him.

'It stops here every month or so, moors for a few hours and then heads either under the metal bridge or towards the canal. He comes in and goes out. The last time I remember seeing it was a month ago. I know exactly as it was on my birthday, that's why I remember. Are you resident?'

He nodded. 'I'll not add to my room, I'll pay. Happy birthday even though it's a little late.'

She smiled. 'Ta. It'll not take long.'

Danny watched her leave, admiring her legs and sipping his beer before scanning the people sitting at the various tables. It was at that precise moment his world stopped and beer dribbled from the corner of his mouth. Screwing up his eyes he studied the person on the furthest table, the one directly above the moored *Arcanum*. It was Matthew bloody Merrill. He was wearing a smart brown leather jacket and sunglasses, but it was him alright. The man he was chatting to was in total contrast. He knew him, too.

* * *

Tony stood looking beneath the gable end of the Phoenix Hotel whilst holding an A4-sized photograph detailing a series of hatched lines. Holding it at arm's length, he could see they matched an area of the mural. His frustration was clearly etched on his face. He believed the idea of interpreting the photographs would not take days, but weeks and he did not have the luxury of time on his side and neither, he believed, had Danny Maynard. His phone rang.

'We have a DNA match for the sleeping bag and other items found where Trevor died. There are others but none is on the database apart from one.'

This last part of the sentence seemed to go astray. 'Was this DNA found at any of the other crime scenes?' Believing they were talking about Danny, Tony was growing more and more confused.

'No. Do you want to know the other link?'

'All ears.'

'Wayne Beales.' There was an extended silence. 'Found on the rucksack and the sleeping bag.'

Tony sighed. 'That's possibly because the two bags came from Beales's house. Did you read my report? His wife's probably in on it, too,' frustration evident in his tone. 'It could be on a few other items at the scene as DNA is easily transferred. The fact that the bags were there tells us Danny was there, but Beales? Anyway, how do you have his DNA?'

'Voluntarily given after the house incident.'

Tony raised an eyebrow, thanked the caller and hung up as

he looked at the street name on the metal plaque opposite him. He knew the DNA given voluntarily could not be used to investigate another crime. His thought process switched.

John Foley, Ringo Foley. He chuckled at the thought. *George Foley and of course, Paul Foley.* Leaning against the mural he rang April.

'The clue we're looking for about Merrill's new name ... just been thinking and something came to me. What if Danny was directing us to The Phoenix but also to the road on which the pub stands, where Merrill got his inspiration, maybe. It's the only building on Foley Street. What do we know of a Foley, particularly when we add any of the first names of the Beatles?' As he asked April, he also questioned his own rationale.

She immediately reached the same initial conclusion as he. 'Ringo Foley?' She chuckled. 'Are you serious?'

'Let's think laterally, not just their stage names but also their real names ... Richard, was the only one to change his first name. There's a reason Danny sent this and we'd be foolish to just pass things by.'

'He's in his twenties, Tony, and he probably doesn't know who the Beatles were, let alone know their original names.'

'True, but let's keep an open mind, as right now we've nothing else. It was just a thought. I often wonder why he just didn't walk in to a station and talk rather than go through this bloody cloak-and-dagger subterfuge, but then, knowing Danny, he's probably up to his neck in whatever it is and the last thing he wants is another spell inside. Beales mentioned he'd said he hated every moment. If he was back in prison, he'd at least be safe and we'd not be wasting so much time.'

* * *

'Secrets or mysteries.' The words spoken over his left shoulder startled Danny back to the present. He turned to look at the waitress. She wore a smile, more in satisfaction than joy. 'I asked Lisa on reception to Google the word *Arcanum*, the name of the boat there. You asked me what it meant.'

'Yes, thank you.'

'I've also brought you your lunch.' She placed the plate before him and handed over cutlery wrapped in a napkin. 'That's what it means, *Arcanum*, it's a pretty name.'

'Thank you again and thanks for the toastie. Looks delicious.'

'As I said, it's my favourite. I wonder what secrets and mysteries that boat holds, certainly doesn't hide its disorder and untidiness.'

Danny laughed and she giggled. 'It wouldn't do for me.' She responded inadvertently by touching his arm but quickly withdrew it. 'Sorry, I don't do chaos, never have.'

'What do they say, where there's muck there's brass.'

'Only if you're a cleaner. Enjoy!' She turned and moved back inside.

On returning his gaze to Merrill he was surprised to see that he had left, but the boatman remained seated with another coffee and disconcertingly, he seemed to be staring in his direction. It was a déjà vu moment, as if he were back on the canal bank, when it was a different time. He was wearing different clothes and it certainly was a different place. As on the previous occasion, the man slowly bowed his head as if acknowledging Danny's attention, before turning his gaze to look over the dark waters of the dock and the Tobacco Warehouse beyond.

Danny ignored the cutlery, picking up part of the toastie. He took a bite suddenly realising how hungry he was. The girl was right. It was delicious. He must get her name. Turning, he scanned the room through the glass wall hoping to glimpse Merrill, but the reflection from the glass prevented clear identification other than for the first few metres. He was not there. It was of little consequence.

* * *

It was getting late in the afternoon. DCI Mason strode into Copy Lane. He was not expected but the latest information he had received caused him to detour. The entry to the building could best be described as tired. He paused for a moment considering how the development recently undertaken to build new police centres showed a real commitment within Merseyside to fighting the crime in a large city and dock. What appeared before him clearly justified that need. The smell of the building never seemed to change.

April Decent was at her desk finishing paperwork for one of the crimes she had been investigating. Her court attendance that afternoon had resulted in a successful verdict and she could now put the case to bed; another criminal behind bars. She was surprised when Mason entered.

'You've not heard and I wanted to tell you personally as this might be the break we need. We have another homeless victim,' he told her without ado.

'Dead?'

Mason shook his head. 'She was found in the early hours of this morning by one of the charity workers beside some waste bins where she'd sheltered. It's away from the usual area.' He moved to the street map on the wall and looked at the locations of the other scenes of crime. Once orientated, he pointed to the spot. 'Younger person this time. Maybe an illegal looking at the clothes, what she was found with and her limited knowledge of English. It certainly wasn't your usual down-and-out. She was interviewed with support from an interpreter. She's Bulgarian. Normally an attack on a young female sleeping rough wouldn't hit our radar but the similarities were flagged within the system. There's also a connection with alcohol. One or two bottles may well have been dropped by one person. There were only the victim's prints so Forensic believe they were wiped before delivery. When he left the bottles, he spoke softly but she could only make out the words 'drink' and 'without'. She suggested it was said too quickly and she was still in a state of sleep. It's when he returned after an hour or so, maybe longer, that she felt an arm wrap around her head and she felt something prick her neck. The speed of her reaction, she feels, threw the person off balance before they fled. That swift response probably saved her life.'

'And her neck?' April responded with eager anticipation.

'A slight puncture wound and a tear. It has been swabbed and will be assessed. The second positive, April, we now have a witness.'

'Whilst you're here, sir, we need to find two people known to us. Danny Maynard, I've mentioned him at our last meeting and a Matthew Merrill, who we believe is now working under an alias. Live Facial Recognition might just winkle them out as we believe they are still in the central area.'

'Are you already using retrospective recognition with respect to your dedicated watch list?'

'Yes, but apart from the one we believed to be positive, the others proved to be false.'

'LFT could just save a life.' April deliberately over dramatized in the hope she would get some response.

'We have to tread warily with biometric data collection as we're too often hounded by requests for the release under the title "public information", as they believe this action will infringe their human rights and freedoms. These are now requested on a regular basis. Batting them away with the excuse, "for national security", will not hold back the flood for long, even though it's a positive tool in our future armoury, just like DNA and finger-prints, in finding the baddies.'

April said nothing more but did not take her eyes from his.

'I'll do what I can, April, but it will be specified areas only and for a limited period. That I can assure you, so you'd better have a vague idea where your boys might be.'

CHAPTER 18

The atmosphere in the hotel reception and bar area in the evening seemed to contrast significantly with the daytime ambience. It seemed homely even for such a large space. Although the lights were on throughout the area, there was still a warmth with the infusion of the day's mellow, fading light and the animation of guests who still sat enjoying the waterside patio. There was a buzz, an excitement, a causerie of small talk that seemed to emanate mainly from the area by the windows. Danny stood for a moment allowing this latest novelty to wash over him, absorbing every nuance his senses permitted. Although he felt intimidated by his inexperience and his uncertainty in such settings, he was savouring every moment.

The receptionist had changed shifts but he was greeted with the same warmth.

'Could you call a taxi for me, please?' Danny asked and gave his room number and surname, Nellist, omitting his first name which he considered to be archaic. It took a moment. The receptionist turned and checked a collection of small portals positioned behind before removing an envelope. 'This came for you this afternoon, Mr Nellist. I take it you are enjoying your stay with us?'

Danny's surprise would have been easy to interpret as he took the envelope. 'Thank you, yes. Wonderful.'

There was no stamp, just a brown envelope on which was written his room number. He tapped it on the back of his hand as he pondered the possibilities.

'Your taxi will only be a few minutes. Please sit over there and I'll call you when it arrives.'

Danny found a seat beneath a huge, framed White Star Line cruising poster. Slipping a finger into the envelope he tore the top before retrieving the note.

> *Have you done as asked?*
> *Did they find the phone?*
> *Don't forget tonight.*

He read it again before slipping it back into the envelope and putting it into the inner pocket of his jacket. His fingers touched the cold metal of the harmonica and he thought about Trevor. His death still puzzled him. Glancing round, he admired the casual clothes of many of the guests – *I need to get some more clothes, better clothes, maybe a suit.* His thoughts were interrupted by the call of his new name.

'Mr Nellist, your taxi is here.' The receptionist pointed to a man standing by the door.

Danny acknowledged his kindness and followed the driver to the car. Within ten minutes they pulled onto Salthouse Quay. It was always a busy location with other cars, but it was the pedestrians who seemed to slow their progress as they meandered from one side of the road to the other.

'Here's fine,' Danny instructed and the taxi pulled to the side. He handed over twenty pounds and held up a hand suggesting the driver should keep whatever change there might be before watching the car leave.

Breathing deeply, he allowed himself a moment's peace before walking between Edward Pavilion and the Dock Traffic Office. The cool of the evening air seemed to funnel within the narrow gap as he found his way onto the side of the Albert Dock. He immediately noted the CCTV cameras dotted strategically along the walkways. He pulled on his old beanie hat and lifted his collar. A brisk walk took him by the Tate. He knew the area like the back of his hand, day or night, as much of his dealing would take place along the waterside that was usually thronged with visitors from every destination. He could often see the world map directly in his mind's eye, the one that was always positioned in front of him, as he heard the many different tongues spoken by tourists. Although he could neither understand nor identify each language, it brought back memories. He could recall not only the names on the map but the colours, the seas and oceans. Looking at the old, masted wooden boats – or were they ships – moored within the dock brought a sadness, a regret of the time he had wasted. He could have been better, sharper. *How many of those ships have travelled from here to the places I saw on that map? How many places have changed in the years since it was published, hung on the wall?* He even remembered the date too – 1968 – and the name Westermann in red set to one corner. The countries of Ubangi and Madagascar sprung immediately to mind for no apparent reason. *Come on, Danny Boy, you haven't got all bloody night. You need food.*

As he walked across Hartley Quay Bridge, the late evening light had mellowed after the sun had set and most of the lights, yellow imitation gas lighting, gave a warmth to the cobbles set before the Piermaster's House, where he leaned against the railings. He was now a tourist, one of many in a popular place. Within minutes, the smell of tobacco drifted into his nostrils, faint and yet at the same time, distinctive. It came with a greater pungency and with it he felt a yearning for a fag. He watched the man cross in front of him, the cigarette set in the corner of his mouth, make his way to the small statue of a figure whose arms were spread as if frozen in a theatrical pose; the quiff and pointing finger added some reality. Danny moved over and stood allowing his own finger to touch that of the statue.

'Billy Fury, but you know that.' The voice behind him was clearly directed at Danny.

Danny turned.

'Before your time, Billy, and before mine. Must have been a great singer to have a statue placed at this historical spot.' Smoke dribbled from the man's nostrils as he continued the impromptu conversation. 'A favour. Could you take a photograph of me with Billy, please? It's always better than a selfie.'

Danny chuckled beneath his breath as he took the man's phone. The flash appeared, bright and immediate, causing a number of people to turn and look as Danny took a second, then a third, before handing back the phone. The man checked the shots.

'Thanks, not bad considering the light.' He took a packet of cigarettes from his pocket and handed them to Danny. 'Take them as a gift. A thank you. It's not full but then life never is ...' He winked, taking a final drag from the cigarette before stubbing it out on the cobbles.

Leaning against Billy Fury, Danny watched the man cross the short bridge over the lock gates as he headed towards Mann Island, leaving Danny weighing the cigarette packet in his hand. He hoped he knew what was inside, but it would wait. Right now, he needed a beer and food, and he fancied Italian.

* * *

Skeeter Warlock threw the leather mannequin, the wrestling dummy that clearly showed its age as well as many battle scars visible across the stained hide, once more over her shoulder with not only ease but a grace and fluidity that seemed to defy her size and proportion. It was a dummy that had been at the club since she was a child. The dummies had even acquired names, names of past coaches and instructors; each was respected and cherished. The smell of sweat, leather and time seemed to mix and fill her nostrils as she held it close, the odour, an infusion, a memory trigger. Skeeter pictured her father, her first instructor, and then the last opponent she had beaten only days before, but as always, she felt as though she were now wrestling with an old friend. What sentimental melancholy she felt as the dummy flew, its single stump leg moving up and over with a grace that soon ceased as the excited sound of the youngsters, the Tumble Tots, moved onto the edge of the brightly coloured mats with an eagerness of noise.

* * *

Michael Peet read the file from the day and made notes on the areas he had been requested to develop. The latest attack on the girl had all the markings of a regular city crime: lone girl, dark doorway, drunken male. It could happen anywhere, sometimes irrespective of the sex of the victim, or age, as anyone could be vulnerable. It had happened on Henry Street, an area of the city that would be busy until late in the evening. Cross-referencing with the other attacks this one, at the outset, did not seem connected. The other attacks were to the west of the city and this was to the east. It was an anomaly only if you disregarded the first death, as that too was disparate and occurred well away from the city. However, investigative policework does not allow convenient selection. The facts must stand and then be acted upon.

For his own curiosity, he wanted to track car registrations alongside the dates of each case but also with the addition of a set time window. He elected between midnight and five in the morning. He also narrowed the search within certain areas of the city. This was fine providing the perpetrator travelled by car, did not live centrally or did not own more than one vehicle. It was a step and the information was already held. For Michael, it was like adding a perimeter fence allowing a check of those coming in and out.

Reading further into the notes made Michael laugh out loud when he read the possible alias for the missing person, Matthew Merrill. 'It's certainly creative if not a tad naïve.' His words fell on deaf ears but the word *naïve* made him pause and swing back on his chair. He looked up the word – naïve – showing a lack of experience, wisdom or judgement – 'Matthew Merrill certainly fitted those categories.' He spoke out loud again. 'If I wanted an alias, how would I find one? Graveyard, cenotaph, street names, buildings and if I wanted to rise like a mythical bird?' He checked Street View for the Phoenix as mentioned and looked at the mural. His fingers tapped the desk as he considered the idea. 'You might just be right, Tony!'

Within ten minutes, he had found three people by the name of Richard Foley in the system. Only one was the correct age category for Merrill. He checked the various resources at his disposal from public records, the electoral roll and the more sophisticated systems held by the national police.

Richard Foley did not own or rent any property in the area. He did not own a car, collect benefit or have a National Insurance number. According to records, he did not exist. Even if he broadened the CCTV search to allow for commuting, nothing showed. 'He's subletting and paying with cash or goods.' It was a typical ploy of drug traffickers. A room in an apartment or an apartment is allocated and the occupant is not registered. Sometimes their stay is unwanted and uninvited, but they are there through threat and intimidation. In other cases, mortgage and bills are paid by the owner, the apartment is looked after and monies for the convenience are transferred overseas. Considering the number of new apartments built within Merseyside over the last few years, there would be many hundred bought for investment and left unoccupied. A small percentage of these might be used to house mistresses or miscreants. The problem was locating them. Removing the wheat from the chaff would need a favourable breeze.

The search for properties they had linked to Danny's photographs so far had proved negative. The next step would be for officers to call to those apartments suspected of maybe harbouring him and hold discussions with the management and security. The first location was the accommodation around the Tobacco Warehouse. Michael added his notes to April's morning epistle before continuing.

* * *

Danny paid his bill and waited outside for a few moments for the taxi to appear. He could not remember the last time he had enjoyed a meal so much. The lasagne was wonderful. He would grab a beer on returning to the hotel and then sleep. The thought of fresh sheets, a hot shower and a coffee, providing he could work out how to add the pods to the machine, filled him with a child-like excitement.

The taxi stopped and he moved from the restaurant door. The flash of a red cycle caught his peripheral vision but disappeared swiftly between two buildings. He pulled a face, thinking of a similar bike that was folded on the front of the boat he had seen on the canal and also below the hotel. He thought nothing more of it as he gave the driver directions.

The reception and bar area of his hotel were still busy. He took his beer outside. There was a breeze that swirled within the confines of the two old buildings. A light shone from one of the three canal boats but the others were in darkness. Danny deliberately looked for the red bike. It was still where he had seen it before. He had had enough of this day and made his way to his room; the cigarette packet now seemed to be burning a hole in his inner jacket pocket.

* * *

Beales lifted the latch on the shed door and moved inside before searching for the light switch. The mug and the plate remained on the worktop amongst the other mess. He knew Danny had been here and looking at the white, cloudy ring resting on the dregs of tea remaining in the mug, it had been a good few hours ago. There were other signs of his presence, not here in the shed but in the house. They were subtle but Wayne had learned to read them; it was his wife's demeanour, her tolerance and her good nature. It was always spring when Danny had been and winter when he had not stayed for a while. That was fine, but he resented the intrusion after he had shown such kindness and so he had ensured there would be a cost.

Moving three tins of used paint, their lids deformed through prising and hammering, revealed a plastic container. Lifting it down he placed it next to the mug. It was more a tithe, a reward, but also a way of paying back. Danny knew nothing of it. He had trusted his neighbourly friend. There was never enough removed for him to notice but enough after a time for his handlers to suspect, question and demand retribution. His innocent protestations fell on deaf ears, before coming to a head.

Checking his watch, he needed to grab a few hours before work. Placing the box and the tins back, he collected the mug and the plate. He thought about Danny's father. 'Bloody hell, he's just like his old man, any port in a storm.' He flicked off the light, yawned and went inside. The house was quiet, other than for the television talking to no one in the lounge. He went to the bedroom.

'How long did the little leech on society stay in my shed?'

His wife stirred from beneath the duvet. 'He left in the morning, just before it was light. He said you went off early, very early. Why?'

'Did he. I'm terrorised and bloody spied on in my own bloody house.'

The words hovered, unheard. Her breathing had changed and a light snore could be heard. Wayne sighed and went downstairs.

CHAPTER 19

*A*rcanum moved back off its mooring. He could see the bottle on the table, slowed the throttle and quickly popped the alcohol into the cupboard. It was another day to be ticked off. There was a slight chill in the air and the familiar blanket of mist clung to the dock's dark surface but the lights from the hotel spread within the boat's wake like spilled cream. A special request had granted travel from Stanley Dock through to Salthouse Dock; a process the weather and traffic allowed. Passing through Collingwood Dock, the boatman lowered a buoy attached to a weighted, large container over the edge of the boat, leaving it as close to the dock wall as possible before turning and passing through into Trafalgar Dock. If it moved within the water, it would not go far and it would be collected within the half hour. There would be no further unscheduled stops until reaching Salthouse Dock. He would receive assistance to move through the dock lock system but they knew him and he them. His passage had been booked in advance. The time was 6.25, a time when Liverpool was at its best. Passing through Sid's Ditch gave the impression of solitude. He breathed the fresh morning salty air. Another job was done, he hoped it would be his last.

* * *

The paper dart flew straight until finally looping and sliding to a halt on Skeeter's desk. It not only impressed Skeeter, it amazed Tony who had launched it.

'Bloody hell, Wicca, that was not only an elegant flight but also a perfect landing. What do pilots call them? Greasers?' He did not wait for a response which was just as well as she did not intend to boost his bloated ego. 'That was certainly one of those. Did you see the way it kissed your desk? The passengers wouldn't even have known they'd landed!' His wide grin endorsed his sense of achievement. 'I'll have that one back to add to my collection of one.' He pointed to Wicca's aircraft which he had secured to the whiteboard.

'Is it a note or just a prototype?' Skeeter queried, already bored by the activity.

'Michael contacted me before he left this morning,' Tony continued. 'That ridiculous piece of detective work that was scoffed at within these four walls may not be so ridiculous after all. He believes there's a strong possibility Richard Foley could well be the alias for the missing Merrill. There's nothing on Maynard either and that's with retrospective facial recognition. If you ask me, Wicca, that technology has a long way to go before we get the accuracy we need, and to think the government wants to embed it into everyday policing, even linked to the personal body cams. They're going to have to tweak those old algorithms a tad more before they'll be of use, and that's if we don't get a massive public outcry about loss of freedoms and human rights abuse.'

'I'm glad he called, as we have Michael's latest thoughts to thank for our elected task today, my friend. We're visiting a few locations near the place the bricks were missing from the wall, you remember the location Kasum discovered early on in the case?' She pointed to the one arranged on his whiteboard before holding up photographs, mug shots, of Maynard and Merrill. 'Going to see if we can shine a light into some dark crevices.'

'Dirty word, crevice. Have I time for a brew?'

Wicca shook her head and grabbed her jacket. 'Nope, not now!'

* * *

The cigarette packet sat next to the harmonica on the desk positioned at the far side of the room. The radio played, as steam from the shower curled delicately from the en suite. Danny was making a rough attempt at singing along. He could not remember the last time he had slept so well, and the thought of a cooked breakfast now fed his every thought.

Although the bathrobe was a little short in the sleeves it was a welcome luxury. Moving to the cigarette packet, he removed the foil, unwrapped it and let the key sit on his hand. The details or what he interpreted to be instructions were written on each remaining cigarette within the pack. One included only a telephone number. He now knew the date, time and when to call. Once each handwritten order had been completed, he could smoke the cigarette. It was a win-win.

'Clothes, I need clothes,' he announced whilst staring into the full mirror. 'Blue, a blue suit. Bloody hell, Danny Maynard in posh clobber. Jeans, and one of those shirts with a horse and rider carrying a hammer.' He immediately took up the pose of Billy Fury whilst lifting his jacket collar.

* * *

Kasum had read the report of the attack on the young woman. She was not only professionally disappointed that the perpetrator was still at large, but emotionally upset by the vulnerability of the victims. Her research into similar cases had drawn a blank. It seemed dead dropouts, vagrants and down-and-outs were found in every town and city throughout Britain, with a higher percentage in the winter months. Understanding those statistics did not require a degree or the mind of a detective constable. Vulnerability was a clear contributor to consider when researching serial killers: the young, the elderly and the infirm. *The Sneinton Strangler*, convicted of killing homeless women was one case she had reviewed whilst checking the psychology of the serial killer. Her research brought back memories of the term *Triad of Evil* – which comprised the three main early traits displayed by potential violent killers – bedwetting, animal cruelty and fire setting. She was not convinced as they seemed to be merely pegs on which to hang a hat. *Had we all not wet the bed at some stage of our lives?*

These deaths, murders, could not be classed as violent, other than the latest and that she believed was owing to circumstance rather than plan. They were all alcoholics and had been for a number of years; their sex and ages differed. None was sexually or physically abused pre or post death, and yet all had a very high concentration of potassium within their system.

Pausing she checked the pathology results for the last victim:

The physical damage to the right side of the victim's neck appears to have been caused by a sharp needle or very fine blade. There is a concentration of potassium chloride beneath the epidermis where there has been a breach of the stratum basale. Owing to a possible struggle or movement there is evidence of a tear and some swelling to the area. There was, from the evidence seen on the victim, a quantity of injected KC. Anything present it is believed was from a contaminated needle.

Toxicology shows the victim had not taken alcohol within the last thirty-six hours. No evidence of illegal drugs was found in two samples taken.

Superficial contusions were observed to the left side of the head as if it has been held forcibly, an indication the head was held to expose the neck.

According to the interview report, two full bottles of strong alcohol had been handed to her earlier. The person just shook her awake and pointed to them. He said something but she did not understand.

Whoever had attacked the girl had made their first mistake. They had made an incorrect assumption and they had failed. Kasum brought up the witness statement and made notes: *Believed to be male. Average height.* She paused when she read the description of his feet: *The victim believed he had blue plastic bags covering his shoes.* Kasum's immediate thought was of disposable shoe covers. She scanned the report for evidence of further protective clothing and quickly found it. Hat, gloves and face covering, again blue, were mentioned.

The killer has planned, prepared and is organised, but what is the motive? To make them comatose before returning? An alcoholic could not say no, but the girl ...

Her thoughts tumbled in her head as she collected her water bottle and stood, allowing her body to stretch before moving to the window. Staring out onto the main road, now heavy with traffic, Danny Maynard came into her mind. She remembered talking about his odyssey, his journey. She crossed the room pausing deliberately at Tony's desk and stared at the photographs. She methodically considered each one whilst narrowing her eyes, trying to comprehend what, and hopefully where, they might be or represent. She stopped at one and removed the bottle from her lips. The photograph seemed to be taken facing down onto a patterned pavement with one carved stone plinth to the left. Owing to the angle of the shot, the perspective seemed distorted.

'I've seen that pattern but where?' She grabbed her jacket.

* * *

Danny stared out of the breakfast room window. The three boats had gone.

'Good morning. Looking for *Arcanum*?' The voice was familiar. The waitress beamed a broad smile. 'Or do you have enough secrets to keep locked in your head for one day?'

Danny felt his face flush. 'Do you want to know a secret, promise not to …?' He sang to the Beatles' tune but it was in the wrong key and sung in a whisper. The waitress looked at him blankly. 'My uncle was a fan of the group. That was his favourite. He used to whistle it to me. Got on my nerves if I'm honest.'

She could see his mood change. 'He's your favourite? Your uncle. I can tell.'

'He's good to me, especially when I was a kid. Do you know that song?' Danny's mood seemed to be lifted by her kind words and presence.

'Sorry, no. We hear all sorts on the speakers in here but I tend to switch off. They drone on with the same stuff hour after hour.'

'Have you seen the statue of Billy Fury by the dock?'

She shook her head. 'Are you ready to order your brekkie?'

Danny laughed. 'Sorry. A full English, please.'

'It won't be long. Help yourself to juices, cereals and the stuff on the side. Coffee or tea?'

'Coffee.'

'By the way, your boat, the one full of secrets and mysteries, left dead early just as I arrived and that was at about six. Went under the metal bridge over there and into the dock system. They don't usually do that in the morning. Must be special.'

* * *

Kasum waited at the lights of North St John Street. They seemed to take an age. The traffic was busier than she had expected and pedestrians seemed quick to dash between cars when stopped. She turned left, hoping her memory was accurate. The A5039 was one way. Stanley Street was to her right. She indicated, waited for two pedestrians and then drove down, parking as soon as possible in a taxi zone. The road pattern was identical to that on the picture from Danny's phone and she felt relieved it was not a wasted journey. Kasum stared at the statue of a woman seated on a stone bench and she checked the design of the plinth legs, they also matched. This was the place. The figure was that of Eleanor Rigby. She read the plaque:

ELEANOR RIGBY
For all the lonely people.

She rested a hand sensitively on Eleanor's head, it was cold and it brought a shudder as the link between loneliness and cold struck her. It seemed so real. She read the words again as the thought of those recently murdered came to mind. There was more written but it was the last line that made her pause.

From the album

Revolver.

Just what is Danny telling us this time? Her finger traced the last word.

She called April. 'It's Kasum. I've discovered another location.'

April moved across to the whiteboard and stared at the collection of photographs. 'Which one?' She paused as Kasum described the picture.

'It could mean Danny is linked with the killing of the homeless or he's directing us to the one who is, Merrill.' Kasum sounded excited by the discovery.

'He seems to be fixated by statues and for a lad whose purportedly as thick as my desk, he seems to have designed some quite subtle clues with professional ease. That's providing these are clues and we are not staring at a mirage.'

Kasum mentioned the word 'revolver' but also questioned its relevance over her belief the clue was really the link to the homeless and not a firearm.

'When Skeeter and Tony return, we need a briefing to consolidate what we have. 15.00?' April paused. 'Why would Danny link anything with the Beatles? He's too young, even though he was brought up here it doesn't naturally follow ...' She stopped. 'Putting you on speaker, Kasum. I'll be a minute.' April went to the notes Tony had filed on the board and flicked through the pages. 'Did you say you are on Stanley Street?'

'Yes, the Rigby statue.'

'Danny's uncle, his maternal uncle, is Stan Nellist. He practically brought the lad up when he was kicked out of his own house, when his father left and other men played musical beds ...'

'Do you want me to pay him a visit?' Kasum seemed eager.

'I'll message the address and meet you there.'

* * *

The red Volvo 4x4 pulled off Regent Road and drove between the castellated dock gates over the tracks that remained from the dock railway. Within minutes, the two young men had dressed in wet suits, goggles, swim caps and gloves. The dockside was quiet and the water looked cold, the colour of wet slate even though the sky was blue. To the right, set within the water were three canoe water polo courts, flotsam in the form of various plastic containers had collected and rippled in one corner. One looked at the other.

'Welcome to Collingwood Dock.'

'Great! Apart, that is, for that fucking old clock. It hasn't worked for ages, why don't they just knock it down and fill this lot in? Make great parking for the footie crowds now the stadium is there.' He pointed to the skeletal, white structure, future home to Everton Football Club.

'The Victoria Tower's an historical piece of architecture, it's known locally as the six-sided dockers' clock. Rumour has it, each clock faced one of the docks but I think that's scouse legend.'

'It could have a hundred bloody sides and it'd still tell the same time day and night on each of its clocks. Have you noticed that they all tell different fucking times,' he sighed and looked again at the water. 'Let's get this over with. After you. It'll be fucking freezing and we'll probably get some kind of STD from swimming in this stuff you describe as water. Looks like a bloody sewer and at times it smells like one, too.'

His partner, a lad of few words, dropped his goggles. 'You're a fucking tart, Briggs.' The last word was said as his feet left the side. The splash was minimal. On surfacing he immediately started a steady crawl towards the red buoy, occasionally glancing back to see if he were still alone. He was not. Briggs had reluctantly slid into the water with the odd protesting groan and had started swimming slowly whilst constantly moaning.

The activity was being observed with interest from the back seat of the car. Collingwood Dock had once been a popular cold water swim zone but now Princes Dock had replaced it. The dark suited swimmers brought the buoy to the jetty dragging with it the attached sunken box. They climbed out lifting the buoy and the container attached to the rope. The whole lot was swiftly placed in the boot of the Volvo. The face looked away before concentrating on his phone, confirming the collection was complete. He could relax.

CHAPTER 20

The empty clothing bags from his morning shop, alongside the newly purchased clothes, underwear, trainers, socks, a sweater and jeans, filled the bed as Danny stood in front of the mirror. The blue suit seemed perfect alongside the light grey polo shirt. He had shaved. His fears of the daylight seemed quite ill-founded, particularly when he was away from his regular haunts and dressed so differently; the sunglasses helped. He knew they were there, and he knew they'd be looking. *Hide in plain sight. They'll not be expecting you and change just enough to make the unsure cautious.* The words came back to him.

'Well, Mr Nellist, you do scrub up proper good, like.' He leaned over and collected the harmonica, lifted it to his lips and gently blew whilst sliding it back and forth. There was something tragic about the improvised cacophony that lacked melody and subtlety, it was more a siren's call but Danny was too busy looking at himself in the mirror to even hear the warning. Before leaving, he collected the cigarette packet, and the butterflies fluttered and filled his stomach. 'You're sailing close to the wind, Danny. Keep your eyes open and your senses keen.' The face in the mirror reflected the same degree of anxiety.

* * *

Kasum was waiting in the car as April pulled in behind. The road was quiet. Kasum moved to April.

'It's hard to believe Maynard came from here, it's not the environment that comes to mind when you read his police record. I believe the uncle felt a degree of guilt when his sister's husband turned out to be a callous bastard, made her life a total misery. Uncle's much older than Danny's mum, she may well have been an afterthought and he was always protective, as was their father. They managed to extract Danny's dad from the house when she'd had enough. Unfortunately, she seemed to attract the abusive and they soon realised they couldn't take responsibility for every failed and aggressive relationship. Allowing Danny to live there with him was the natural and logical answer.'

'I understand the uncle is infirm.'

'Industrial injury, worked in the chemical industry in Birkenhead and received early retirement in his late forties, on ill-health grounds, from what we've discovered. The house was paid for from the compensation he received.'

'His wife?'

'Left him before the accident. No children.'

April rang the doorbell and it took a while before Stanley Nellist opened the door. The sound of a Beatle's tune could be heard in the background. Kasum turned to April and raised her eyebrows. 'That's positive at least!'

'DI Decent and this is DC Kapoor. May we come in? It's about Danny.'

His head lowered and they both noticed the transparent pipes running over his ears and disappearing into each nostril. 'What have the nosy busybodies said he's done this time?' His frustration was clear and there was a hint of anger in his tone.

'As yet, nothing, but he may need our help as he's been attacked twice, but I think you know that. He's also left the police a number of clues, but as to what and why we are unsure.'

'Danny?' His uncertainty was clear.

Within minutes they were sitting in the lounge. It was orderly and clean.

'What do you mean left you clues?'

April removed the photographs and passed them over to him. She deliberately left the pictures of the cash and the guns as part of the group. 'These were on a phone we believe he left for us to find. He rang 999 and suggested he was in grave danger.'

Nellist looked through the photographs, pausing at some longer than others. 'His photography's not improved much. What's with these?' He held up the ones showing the money and the guns.

'We don't know. However, we've interpreted some and they do make sense providing we are on the right track. Did Danny like Beatles' music?'

For the first time since their arrival, they noticed an immediate change in his demeanour and a smile appeared on his lips. 'The best band in the world, ladies, and they're ours, scousers, and the boys have always been proud of their roots. Do you know, I met Ringo? It was years ago when I was a kid. He was going through the airport with his wife, Barbara. I'd been plane spotting. Never forget it. He stopped and posed for a photograph. I still have it. He's my favourite and he's still alive.' He pretended to play the drums.

'DI Decent plays the drums too,' Kasum mentioned in the hope of breaking the barriers that obviously existed.

'Is that right? The drummer is the heartbeat of the band in my opinion. The engine house.' He beat his imaginary sticks again.

April nodded and thought the information about Ringo

supported the possible alias of Merrill and this snippet gave it more credence. 'Would Danny know exactly who Ringo was?'

'Goodness me, yes. I taught him well.'

'One of the pictures.' Kasum leaned over as she selected it. 'That's part of the statue of Eleanor Rigby and Danny deliberately added it. As you know, it's on Stanley Street. We thought he might be directing us back to you. Has Danny left anything else here other than clothes and some personal items?'

Nellist leaned down and selected the two photographs showing cash and guns. 'Like these personal items? Is that what you're suggesting?' His protective defiance had made a swift reappearance.

'Yes. We're of the belief that Danny may have taken items, those items, from the people with whom he was linked. That's why he's been attacked. We think they will try to kidnap him and make him tell them where these things are. They'll not harm him seriously until the items are found and returned. Has anyone been here asking similar questions? Remember, we are on Danny's side in this matter.'

There was a pause and he adjusted the flow on his oxygen before taking two deep breaths. He nodded. 'Two, one was a big lad, and I mean big. Came in a big car, I think it might have been a Volvo. Let's just say they persuaded me to let them search the house, which they did thoroughly. Garage, loft, everywhere. They found nothing. He had some drugs, but not much and they tossed them on that table.'

'Did they harm you?' April asked.

'No but they said they would if the goods, that's what they called the stuff, the goods were not recovered. They left the place tidy and were courteous as well as frightening at the same time.'

April removed another photograph and placed it in front of Stanley. 'Take a careful look at this man.'

Stan held it at arm's length before bringing it closer to his face. 'That's one of them, the smaller of the two. He did the talking and made the threat. Strangely, he was also polite and calm. Told me he was Danny's mate and had been for some years and he only wanted the best for him.'

'When was this?'

'When you're in the house constantly, days just meld into one. Last week. Weekends are no longer on my natural calendar. I couldn't say for certain, sorry. That's the truth.'

It was Kasum who put the question that struck the target. 'Could he have stashed it at your neighbour's house? He was close to Wayne.'

Stanley laughed. 'Close to Wayne? Do me a favour. He was close to his missus more like. To put it politely, ladies, she's been seducing him for years. It's as plain as day to anyone apart from that daft husband of hers. When he went out to work, Danny went in. Maybe Wayne doesn't want to see it. I have to admit though, Wayne's been kind to Danny since he was a nipper. Loads of patience.'

'What do you know about potassium chloride, Mr Nellist, as you were once in pharmaceuticals?'

The question clearly came out of left field and immediately stifled any developing trust there might have been. Nellist looked at the two women in turn. The frown said much and the silence was audible.

'Sorry, but what's that got to do with our Daniel?'

'He was at a crime scene where the person died from an injection of that very chemical.'

Stanley laughed out loud, bringing his hand to his nose to secure the nasal canula. 'He doesn't know his arse from his elbow. Kill? Injecting?' He paused. 'I was going to say drugs but then we all know he dabbled. Potassium chloride, known as potassium salt, odourless, colourless and highly soluble. It's used in the manufacture of fertilizer amongst other things but also used in the food industry, but you know that as I was in the fertiliser business until ... Anyway, that was a long time ago and since then, me and this oxygen bottle don't stray far. Like all chemicals, in the right hands they are marvellous but in the wrong hands ...'

'Did you talk much to Danny about the stuff?'

'You have to remember that Danny could forget faster than his teachers could teach. What went in here came immediately out of here.' He demonstrated with his hands. 'If I did, it would be forgotten almost immediately but I didn't, I had no reason. Danny still thinks fertilizer is shit from cows and horses. Does that answer your question?'

'Yet he knew the names of capital cities and their countries.'

'And a bloody lot of good that's done him. He's never been further than fucking Blackpool to the north, that was when he was ten, he threw up on the big dipper thingy, Manchester to the east and Chester to the south. Although he knows where the Isle of Man is, to him, it's an exotic Island.'

April turned to Kasum and then back to Nellist. 'Thanks for your time. If Danny comes here, please let us know, or if you see him next door. We'll see ourselves out.'

They left and paused by the cars.

'"The Graduate" – Mrs Robinson has a far better ring to it than Mrs Beales!' April's tone was disapproving. 'I wonder when the seduction started. A minute.' April walked down the Beales's driveway and knocked on the door as hard as possible. There was no answer. There was also no car. He was at work but her, his missus? 'Let's hope she was out and not with Danny.'

CHAPTER 21

Skeeter and Tony sat in the briefing room along with Kasum. They were comparing their day's progress.

'The statue. Who'd have thought he'd know about the Beatles and link it with his uncle?'

'That may well consolidate Tony's theory, particularly if Danny knew of Merrill's visit. He didn't give a name from what Nellist said. Danny may well know he couldn't get rid of Merrill on his own but he could try to get rid of him another way.' Skeeter seemed enthused by the whole saga. 'An odyssey to remove a thorn from his side, for both himself and his uncle, and whatever he has, to keep for himself.'

Tony rubbed his face with his hand. 'Why not send an anonymous message to us saying where we could find Merrill, why this stupid charade?'

Skeeter looked at Tony unsure if he knew what the word meant. 'Trust? If Danny has set this up, he may well be watching. Has he seen you, Tony, at the mural, you, Kasum, at the statue? When he feels the time is right, he may then spill the beans.'

Tony turned his collar up and made a gun shape with his fingers. 'Remember, Wicca, we're talking about Danny Maynard and not 007.' He rolled his eyes and blew over his finger ends, at the same moment as the door opened and both Decent and DCI Mason entered. The room fell silent as they took their seats.

'Good afternoon. I want to start with some information, info that has eluded us since the start of the killings. It concerns Mr Felix Spencer. You've read the details on file. As you are aware, we knew very little until we discovered a relative. It's been confirmed that his last rental property was in Norbury in Staffordshire. We understand he had a fascination for not only the booze, but also canal boats. Bit of an anorak from all accounts. Norbury Junction is a busy area for boats, and it's believed he helped out there. He would also hop on boats wherever possible, for the day mainly, but if the opportunity arose when help was needed, he could be away for a few days.'

'What did they do with the drunken sailor?' Tony's lack of enthusiasm was clear.

'A whole new meaning to hitchhiking. Novel,' Kasum said tapping him on the arm.

'Apparently, the local force interviewed a few people at the wharf and it's not uncommon with the free spirits of the canal boat world, those who are trying to leave the reality of life and take on something a little less brisk and bureaucratic.' Mason checked his notes. 'Apparently, he was last seen heading north on a boat that stopped for services and that was about four months ago, but no one was really sure of the timescale. The key is, we have a relative and they are aware, and progress can be made to release the body for cremation. We also have more forensic details from Victoria's crime scene, but we don't have any background as there are no links with the DNA register. However, there is nothing there to link Danny Maynard, neither were there any forensic traces at any other sites other than that of Trevor Robinson. Formal identification has taken place as his wife has been tracked and she has formerly identified the body.

He's an ex-teacher and musician who succumbed to drugs and drink a number of years ago. According to his wife, their relationship became strained because of his unreasonable behaviour. They tried to sort things out but the booze always won. She hadn't seen him for over two years and has a new partner who is aware of her past. He was with her when she identified the body. The other death has also been identified formally, leaving only Victoria outstanding. It never ceases to amaze me how quickly individuals can be lost in today's society.'

'I take it forensics have no idea regarding the deaths so I wonder how the victims were selected?'

'No, other than what you know, but they died in the same way. They were all alone, down-and-outs with a serious alcohol and drug dependency, apart from the last victim who has made progress and is on her way home.' Mason sighed and tapped the papers on the desk to straighten them.

'She believes the attacker was male, medium height. We also know he was prepared when committing the crimes as he was seen wearing PPE and killing in the same way. He's still out there. There's no forensic link to just one individual for each crime scene, so he's extremely cautious and clever or just bloody lucky.'

'Looking at some of the places where the bodies were located, I'm amazed overshoes wouldn't be torn to pieces owing to the glass and the sharp surfaces found on the ground in the area.' Skeeter added.

'Maybe wearing double or triple. I've seen CSIs do that, depending on the conditions under foot and where step plates would be ineffective.'

Skeeter and Tony ran through their investigations of various occupants at the selected apartments, which had brought them little success.

Tony continued. 'The photographs on the police socials of

Danny and Merrill had resulted in a number of possible sightings, but they have proved to be false. That is not unusual.'

'I feel it's worth pursuing enquiries with Mrs Beales after the revelation from Nellist about a relationship. Make an appointment to see her when her husband is working, it might be good for leverage. Ensure she understands it's not a request. We might appear to be flapping about and rudderless, but things are coming together. Let's get both cases tied up as quickly as possible. Resources cost, let's remember that.' Mason grumbled.

Skeeter stifled a yawn. She wished she had a pound for every time Mason preached that.

The briefing ended and a keen sense of frustration hung in the air. Loose ends had been sorted but no real progress had been made.

* * *

Danny slipped into his uncle's house. Stanley was neither impressed nor happy.

'What's with the suit, you getting fucking married or going to a funeral? If it's the latter, it's all wrong.'

Danny giggled but it was only to cover his anxiety. 'It's new. Just needed to look better. You always suggested that, if you remember.'

'I do, but that's when you never washed or changed your underpants for a week. You look like a pimp. Besides trainers and a suit don't go.'

'You don't say that when McCartney wears the same.'

Stan muttered. He was right of course, so he let it drop.

'Besides, I've had enough of playing second fiddle.'

'And the cash, the cash I take it that is in one of the pictures you left for the coppers?'

Danny frowned but then he realised the police were following the scent. 'They came here, the Rigby statue?'

Stan frowned. 'Just what the fuck are you playing at and why involve me?'

'Did you mention Ringo Starr?' Danny bobbed holding Stan's knees and looked directly at his uncle, an eagerness in his question.

'Was that wrong?'

'Bloody perfect.'

'The money. You've nicked it and the firearms too?'

Danny nodded.

'That's why two guys called and searched this place and also threatened me if what they were looking for didn't turn up. It was only when the police called, judies, too, did I realise what the stuff was. You're out of your depth, lad, and if you play with fire, you're going to get your fingers burned and maybe mine too. Remember, that if you care for me at all, you'll keep me out of this.'

'Is Wayne out? There's was no car when I arrived.' Danny moved the net curtain and checked the drive again. It was still empty.

'They went out when he came in from work. Shopping I'd imagine.'

'I'll not be long.'

Danny slipped off his jacket and felt the harmonica in the pocket. He handed it to Stan. 'See if you can get a tune from that.' Grabbing a towel from the kitchen he slipped over the fence and into the shed. Spreading the towel on the floor he stretched beneath the workbench and retrieved the plastic pipe. He brushed down his polo shirt sleeve and collected the towel, partially wrapping the pipe with it before returning to his uncle's. The tune from the harmonica was clear.

'Bloody hell, Uncle Stan, that's brilliant. I didn't know you played.'

'I had one years ago. Used to love Spaghetti Westerns and the tunes were full of the harmonica. I bought one and practised. When I had the accident, the doctors encouraged me to continue playing it saying it would strengthen my lung capacity. Listen to this.' The tune seemed discordant but scary and disturbing at the same time. Danny was spellbound. When he stopped, Stanley was breathing heavily.

'Bloody marvellous. I didn't know. Why didn't I know you could play?'

'I found it affected my breathing so I chucked the harmonica away. It was good to play that. Funny how it came back.'

'Beatles' tune?'

Stan laughed. 'No, it's called, "Once Upon a Time in the West" by Ennio Morricone. You'll not have heard of him.'

Danny opened the top of the tube and brought out a plastic pack of money, selecting a wedge of notes and placing it on the coffee table. 'For you, Uncle Stan. One day I hoped to pay you back for all you've done for me. I know this isn't a lot but I want you to know without you, your kindness and support I might ...' He moved forward, leaned and hugged the man before him. 'I've never said this to you before, Uncle Stan, but I love you.'

'Mind my tubes you soft mop. Be away with you.'

'Could you ring for a taxi for me? Say it's to go into town if they ask.'

'Cupboard love, I knew it, Danny.' He dialled. 'It'll be five minutes.'

'Play that tune again, please.' He slipped on his jacket as Stan started to play the tune again, until he was interrupted by the blast of a car horn: the taxi.

'Take care and make sure I don't get another visit from ...' He did not finish as he heard the door close. 'He'll be the bloody death of me, that lad.'

As the taxi pulled away, Wayne Beales's car approached his drive. He looked into the back of the taxi but failed to recognise the occupant.

'Did that come from Stan's?' Wayne turned to his wife.

She just shrugged her shoulders. 'You need some sleep; you were out again early this morning and look at the time now. I'll cook you something before you go up.'

* * *

April and Skeeter pulled up outside the Beales's house. The car was in the drive but the curtains were drawn in the upstairs room. Skeeter knocked forcefully. Mrs Beales opened the front door. 'DS Warlock and DI Decent,' she showed her ID. 'Is your husband at home?'

'He's in bed. He's on earlies. Can I help?'

'It's you we need to see, it's of a sensitive nature. It's about Danny Maynard.'

Her face flushed and she looked down. 'What's he done this time?' She turned to look down the hallway nervously.

'We can talk in the car if it helps but, be assured, we are going to talk now.'

She nodded and moved onto the drive towards the car. Once settled, April cautioned her. 'We're not arresting you but you need to be aware of the seriousness of the situation in which you find yourself.'

'How long have you been having sex with Danny?' Skeeter did not prevaricate.

There was a pause before Mrs Beales looked directly at both officers in turn. 'Since he was eighteen. We hadn't got him a birthday pressie so I thought why not?'

'It continued until?' April quizzed.

'The week he burst into the house. When Wayne went to work Danny would pop in.' She giggled. 'Pardon, no pun intended.'

'What did you do for him?' Skeeter's question was spoken deliberately slowly.

'That!'

'No, the sex was for you. We know you did things for him. What did you hide, hold, keep safe?'

'Has he told you?'

Both officers remained silent.

'He'd hand over packages, some small others larger. They were easy to hide. He'd also hide himself on occasion, in the shed. Wayne knew he was there. Providing he didn't take anything or touch his things, he allowed it. He liked Danny.'

'He never knew about you two?'

'Maybe, Wayne had difficulties in that department and he wouldn't seek help. He said it was to do with an incident when he was a school kid but he refused to talk about that as well.'

'So, he never consummated your marriage?'

'Yes, it wasn't then, it was just as he got older, he seemed to have greater difficulty. I still had needs. I tried to help him but whatever I did had little effect. He seemed elsewhere – that was usually in front of the bloody telly, at work or snoring. Don't get me wrong, he's a good man. He just has his demons, like us all.'

'What was in the packages Danny asked you to hold?'

'I don't know, and I didn't want to know. Probably drugs. I know it was wrong, I'm sorry. I didn't want to lose him.'

'Are you holding anything now?' Skeeter asked.

She shook her head. 'No, not for a while. Is he alright?'

'I know you were concerned for his safety after the incident you experienced here. The bad news is he hasn't been seen, even though all our feelers are out. That could be a good thing but also … There will be consequences for your holding goods, as we believe they were class A drugs.'

'Prison?' She looked suddenly pale; concern was clearly etched on her face.

'That's not for us to say. You have been very co-operative and that's in your favour. There is no need for us to mention this to Wayne providing we have your assurance you will inform us immediately Danny comes here.'

'I think he was here this afternoon, next door. I'm sure I saw him leaving in the back of a taxi.'

Skeeter left the car and went to Stan's door. It took a while for the door to open. She held up her ID. 'DS Warlock. Merseyside Police. What time did Danny leave, Mr Nellist?'

'Two hours ago, maybe a little more. You're not from here, woollyback is my guess.' There was defiance in his tone. 'Never trust a woolly particularly if they are with the bizzies and ugly and googly eyed to boot. Just fuck off and leave us in peace.'

Skeeter never let her face slip but moved past him and his zimmer and entered the lounge. The harmonica sat on the coffee table alongside a wedge of twenty-pound notes. Nellist protested breathlessly as he followed her in.

'You've no fucking right. You were not invited in here and more to the point, you're not welcome. You need a bloody warrant.'

Skeeter removed her phone and photographed the items on the table before getting evidence bags from her inner pocket.

'Take the fucking things!'

She nodded as she collected both the harmonica and the cash. 'That's a lot of cash to have hanging about, Mr Nellist. Is it yours?' She had a good idea from where the harmonica had come.

'It bloody well is, yes. You have no bloody right.' He slumped

MALCOLM HOLLINGDRAKE

into his chair and adjusted the oxygen flow trying to control his breathing.

'If that's the case, our forensic accountants will check your finances, your income, benefits, bank accounts and they'll confirm that. Unless, of course you won it or received it as a gift.' Skeeter never let her eyes leave his. 'You play this, too?' She did not allow him time to answer. 'You can't breathe in without gasping but you can blow a tune. Amazing that. How long have you had this?'

'Evil woman. Christ, even your eyes show all the badness in the world. God made you look like that for things you did in a past life. Picking on a sick man who's done no wrong is just pure bleeding evil. What was your name? Warlock did you say? I bet you weren't related to Archbishop Derek.'

'Different spelling and we're from different ends of the spectrum when it comes to comprehending bullshit. I understand it, have a built in oxyometer, it measures the amount of bullshit that comes from the mouths of the guilty. They give us all one when we train for this job. Let's see what reading it registers when I ask you this simple question: are these yours or Danny's?'

Stan hesitated, unsure of the answer he should give.

'Obviously they're fucking yours now you evil—' He did not finish.

CHAPTER 22

The taxi had dropped Danny at the entrance to Salthouse Quay, the two stone gateposts, sentinels to the area. He paid and collected the towel-wrapped length of pipe from next to him on the back seat and brought it to his chest. There had been little conversation between him and the driver, apart from the odd comment on their football allegiance and the weather. He watched the car leave before turning to move out onto the main road.

Danny removed the key from the packet and also a cigarette. He read the instruction printed along its length and checked the location. The building that stood opposite was Canning Place Police Station and he had heard it was soon to close. He was at the correct spot. Balancing the tube between his knees, he took out a lighter and lit the cigarette. Inhaling deeply, he closed his eyes. The nag of nerves still fluttered in his stomach. This area was too exposed for comfort. The edge of the quay was blocked by a chain fence and a gate was positioned at the corner. He looked along the length that ran down parallel to Strand Street, at the equally spaced mooring bollards that no longer served a purpose other than to remind the observer of a time gone by.

Moving to the gate, he flicked the half-smoked cigarette over the edge hoping it would find the water. He removed the key from his pocket, taken from the cigarette packet earlier. The instruction told him it was a Canal River Trust key, and it would unlock the gate allowing access to the line of pontoons that stretched along two sides of the dock. *Arcanum* was relatively easy to spot as he walked down the steps. A wisp of smoke curled from the chimney. It was the fifth boat in the line. Walking along the jetty seemed strange and his blue suit seemed totally incongruous within this setting; his old clothes would have been more suitable, particularly considering the general condition of the boat that was before him.

'Took your time. Getting used to hotel life are we, Danny? Come aboard. You look like a bloody pimp in that suit.'

'"Change enough to make the unsure cautious," that's what you told me.'

'Enough does not mean to go over the bloody top, for Christ's sake. All these tranklements make you look like a tart!'

It was clear he had not changed. He never did have a good thing to say to Danny when he was a kid and now the first words from his lips were still critical and cruel. No welcome, thanks or kiss my arse – it was ever thus. Danny looked at the man's hands; they seemed smaller than those that had often brought him pain and anxiety all those years ago.

'Get aboard, son. I see you've brought it.' He looked at the pipe. 'Is it all there?'

'Most of it. I took some, gave some to Uncle Stan and paid the hotel costs, as you know.'

Speaking back usually ended in a sharp slap but over the last year or so Danny had seen a reluctance in his father to challenge him, maybe a weakness. Perhaps the fact that he was facing a man rather than a child had a direct impact on his aggression, or was it he was just getting older and tired?

Jimmy Maynard took the tube and went inside the boat. The bottle, still unopened stood on the table. Danny followed but glanced at the photograph of himself trapped behind the Perspex. How old was he when that was taken? Twelve? He could not remember. It warmed him to see it there, almost in homage or regret. Maybe he thought more of him than he could ever say, and Danny would ever know. On entering, he looked at the bottle: the inner demon that had driven his parents apart. He stopped and his father saw his hesitancy.

'Over three years and four months, ever since I started to run this slow boat county line. That's the same bottle you always see. Check, you put your initials on it twelve months ago.'

Danny picked it up and he was right. The letters DM and a date were marked on the label.

'Now put it in the cupboard until tomorrow. You can never rest from a demon, believe me. We've a long day ahead of us.'

* * *

Richard Foley sat on the sofa, a coffee before him and the wrapped package, recently retrieved from the dock, sat next to it. The plastic container had been disposed of. Two people sat opposite. The apartment displayed all the hallmarks of its past: the barrel-shaped brick roof, the iron window frames. The light grey painted walls were enhanced by the nautical-themed furnishings, especially the large, historical sepia photographs of the very building in its working heyday. They filled the walls. The mezzanine floor, reached by wrought iron steps and supported on original iron columns, gave a lofty ambience with a hint of modernity. It was luxury in an area that still bore many signs of decay. Some described them as beauty spots on a hag's face but the area was changing and quickly, it would soon be the most fashionable place to live in the city.

'How they get fucking pleasure from swimming in that goo hole beats me. It's full of crap, quite literally. Bad enough swimming for that.' Briggs pointed to the package. 'If I come down with some dreadful disease you know why,' he grumbled.

The smaller of the two said nothing but he raised an eyebrow at Foley as he silently mouthed the word 'dick!'

Foley also said nothing. He stared at the tightly wrapped cube. 'It's paid for and needs selling before the boat returns. Unless we can get our fucking hands on that stealing little bastard and retrieve what's rightfully ours, that's all we have and this place doesn't pay for itself.'

'There's a rumour come through he was back at his uncle's place, you know who? The police have also been, twice in fact. One, a judy, went in and was in a while. Two also went next door but they didn't go in the house. The wife was interviewed in the car outside.'

Foley sat forward and frowned. 'Outside in a car?'

There was a confirming nod. 'That was after our Danny had been? According to our snout anyway, and she's usually on the ball, boss.'

* * *

Mrs Beales stood with her hands on the kitchen sink; the dripping marigolds she had put on the stand looked as though they were praying. She stared at the birds fighting over the remnants of food within the feeder but she was not there, her mind filled with the conversation she had conducted with the police, and she felt sick.

The sound of movement upstairs brought a greater anxiety as she wondered if he had heard the knock, looked out and seen her go to the car. She moved to the kettle, filled it and got his cup ready.

* * *

Skeeter perched on the edge of the desk. 'Admitted both the money and the harmonica belonged to Danny. They were a gift, a thank you for what he does for him. Did you also know he loves the very bones of the lad and it's wicked folk like us that give him a bad reputation. The fact he steals, deals, lies and cheats is in his eyes irrelevant. We're running rapid DNA tests to see who's handled the items. I don't believe Nellist even touched them, let alone blew the harmonica.'

April popped her head around the door. 'We have a warrant to search both properties. Two teams are organised and standing by for early tomorrow morning when he's at work. Tony, you'll be seeing Nellist, as one person here has already upset him enough. Skeeter.' She paused for emphasis. 'Your team is visiting Beales. Let's hope you don't catch anyone in a compromising position. Here, 4 a.m. sharp.'

CHAPTER 23

'I'm absolutely knackered. Why is sleeping in the afternoon so damn difficult?' Wayne shuffled into the kitchen, his plaid dressing gown roughly tied at the waist, his hair in total disarray. He yawned and farted as he pulled out a chair and sat at the table.

'Excuse you and what ever happened to good afternoon?' She placed a mug of tea in front of him. 'What do you want to eat?'

'Good afternoon. Do you know what? I'm not hungry. Who called? Not that bloody Danny, I hope. Thought they were coming through the front door they banged so hard?'

'It was the police. They wanted to speak to me about a private matter and they also wanted to know if we'd looked after anything for Dan.'

Wayne swivelled on the chair running his hand through his thinning hair. 'And?'

'I said what you've said to them. We held things trying to do him a favour not knowing what they were. Good neighbours are what we've always tried to be. They've still not seen or heard from him.'

'He's about. Snakes live in long grass and pop out when you're least expecting them and they bite you on the arse. That's Danny all over. Bitten the bloody hands that's fed him since he was … Anyroad, what's all this about private? I wondered why you sat in the car with them.'

'You were spying on me all along! You really are despicable.' She removed her apron and threw it on the table in front of him. 'I need some air.'

'You'll tell me when you come back, don't you worry about that. I'll know if you're telling the truth.'

* * *

'We have forty-eight hours. You need to clear everything from the hotel room and come here. You do not go back to Stan's and you certainly don't go back next door. You come here and you stay here. If things work out, as I hope they will, we'll be away, with, not only this little lot …' he pointed to the pipe, 'but we'll also have this.' He removed a carrier bag containing a large collection of mixed notes. 'There's a tidy sum, trust me, and if we get back what Merrill paid for the goods and then the cavalry in the form of the police arrives afterwards at his place … Whatever happens, we still have all this. I'm getting too old for this, Danny, and my bottle of luck has been supped nearly to the bottom. We'll have enough, enough for the two of us.'

Danny looked across at his father. He had the same look in his eyes he would have when he came home drunk. It was a cocky kind of arrogance, as if he was right and nothing would stop him. He remembered his mother trying on more than one occasion, and getting not only verbal abuse, but often the back of his hand until she was on the floor.

* * *

It's been just over a year since he found me again. First he found Merrill; then he found me. Once out of prison, Merrill rose from the flames as Richard Foley, then when I got out he took me under his wing. Drugs came, were collected, distributed 'by the slow boat' he always said, which wasn't ships coming from abroad, in at the docks, as I first thought. Later, I knew the truth. Discovering the boatman, Jimmy, was Dad – well, I had mixed feelings about that. He'd always been a user but was mainly an abuser. He'd get what he wanted without a thought for those around him; his own flesh and blood meant nothing. I hated the man. I was taller and stronger then – I could return the blows and abuse and make him pay for the way he broke me and my family.

But when I met him by chance down by the dock, things seemed different, like looking in a fractured mirror, things were distorted and unreal. I could see the traits in me that had been handed down from the man looking into my face. The next time we met it was the same place, by Billy Fury – who had also shown that angry trait. He'd hugged in that same old way, just like after that beating on the fishing trip down the canal when he'd gone to help some woman look for her dog. That had been the guilt and worry in case I said something to mum. He'd smelled the same too – funny how smells unlock memories – but the grey in his hair and beard and the weathered face showed his age. Us meeting then was probably a coincidence.

* * *

Jimmy pointed to the healing wounds on Danny's head and then the pipe, before putting the teabags into cups and bringing the kettle off the stove.

'So, this was the reason for the beatings they dealt you?'

'Yes. If they caught me, they'd make me tell them where it was stored, and I realised once they knew, I'd end up in the

Mersey. They said I'd robbed them well before I took all of that but I hadn't, I took nothing. They said I was slicing cash and goods, not a lot, but enough. I realised it was usually after I'd left stuff with Uncle Stan or Beales but I couldn't work out who it might be.'

'What about the bitch you've been shagging all these years?'

Danny frowned wondering how he knew but then laughed. 'Really? How do ...'

'Really, Danny. How do you know it wasn't her if she was holding stuff. You need to learn that not everyone's who they say they are.'

Danny shot a look at the man opposite. Not a truer word had been spoken.

'If anyone asks from now on, I'm James Forsythe, and Jimmy only to friends. You are now, therefore, Daniel Forsythe when the pilot comes aboard to take us up the Mersey. He's booked for the day after tomorrow as the weather is set fair. That's who I am.' He turned and smiled. 'A new start, a clean page. I've been Forsythe since I bought the boat, that's who he knows. You'll probably never need to call me by my last name and by keeping our first names saves any cockups as it's one less thing to remember.'

'Just another bloody phoenix,' Danny mumbled.

Jimmy heard it but ignored it.

'You could never swim when I was a kid, or that's what you said, so why live on and use a boat?'

'Still can't. Life is all about risk. Who dares wins, as they say. Drink your tea and then go and sort out your hotel room, keep your head down although wearing that suit makes you stand out like a ...' He did not finish but shook his head. 'Get a taxi from the top. There's a small case there for your stuff should you need it. It's clean.'

Within twenty minutes, Danny walked into the hotel. For the first time since his arrival, he felt as though he fitted in. He nodded to the receptionist as he headed for the lift. The suit gave him confidence, a realisation that, in the correct clothes, he was no different from the rest.

The waitress he had chatted to on two previous occasions had noticed him enter, surprised by the change not only in his attire but his overall confidence. She watched as he moved towards the lift. There was clearly a look of surprise on her face and he would have seen it had he turned and noticed.

Within forty minutes, he emerged again into the foyer and stopped by the large model of the *Titanic* trapped within a Perspex display case, whilst he arranged the shopping bags and the suitcase.

'Are you leaving us?' The voice was soft and carried with it an air of disappointment.

Danny turned, immediately recognising the waitress. 'Oh! Hi, yes. You'll never believe it, but I've managed to secure the temporary use of a dockside flat whilst the repair work is carried out at home. Luckily, I have a good insurance company. I'll miss this place.' He lied with ease.

She smiled and lowered her head. 'Did you find your secret boat?'

He laughed. 'Our secret boat. Yes. In my dream last night.'

She blushed. 'I don't usually do this, I mean, I never do this but if you want, you might not, but if you do you could call me and maybe we could have a drink together.' She handed him a piece of paper. 'Helen, my name's Helen. And you?'

'Da... He stopped himself as the word 'cockup' immediately came to mind. 'Stan, short for Stanley but I prefer Stan. Bit old fashioned but then I didn't pick it. Named after an uncle.'

'What were you going to say or had I got you tongue-tied?'

He laughed again as she'd given him an escape route. 'It's not often a pretty girl asks me for a drink.' He looked round and found the clock above the reception desk. 'Sorry, I must dash. Lovely meeting you and thanks for this. I will call.' He tucked the note containing her number into his jacket pocket before making his way to reception. There was nothing outstanding to pay, and within ten minutes he was waiting for a taxi.

CHAPTER 24

K asum's fascination with the photographs showed no signs of abating. There remained only a few still requiring interpretation. It had been her teacher at the evening yoga class she attended who had lent fresh eyes to the dilemma. Perusing the images, she had paused at one, predominantly green apart from the edge of a small, yellow element.

'Those are wellingtons, Kasum, wellington boots, or should I say it's a tiny part of one. It's a close-up shot, maybe even one taken accidentally. We've all done it but they usually turn out blurred and confusing. This, however, looks clear and intentional, that's my guess anyway.'

Kasum had pondered the idea and had come to the conclusion she was on to something. A different perspective was welcome when she had contemplated the image for so long without success. When her mother struggled with a jigsaw, it was often easy for others to walk by, select a piece and put it in the correct place. 'I get blind to the obvious,' was her mother's usual retort. It was the same with this. *So, what do we have in Liverpool that's dedicated to a wellington boot?* She knew about the column situated at Commutation Row, dedicated to the Duke of

Wellington but that seemed too obvious and besides it was at a busy location. Then there were the Wellington Rooms but they were derelict and locked up to protect the structure from further decay. Moving over to the map of the city, she followed the Mersey from the estuary mouth allowing her finger to run down the edge of the land. She paused briefly at the Tobacco Warehouse and thought of the first photograph she had deciphered of the wall with the missing bricks. The residents of the apartments that were occupied had been checked and there was nothing untoward, all seemed legitimate. Moving her finger just a little further, she stopped.

'Trafalgar Dock. Did he fight at the battle of ...?' she mumbled out loud. She googled – 'It was a sea battle and I guess they didn't need wellies for that!' Her heart sank a little, until running her finger further along she paused at Waterloo Dock. It seemed so obvious. She picked up her phone. 'I'm sure, Tony, it's blindingly obvious, once you see it. Many of the apartments along Waterloo Road are rentals, which means you might have possible, illegal sublets, making the tracking of the anonymous tenant difficult.'

Tony's response was enthusiastic. Maybe another piece of the jigsaw had been found and was ready to slot into place. There was certainly a frisson of excitement as Kasum added the details to the board. 'There's one thing we can check, the listing history of the properties, which will show the dates they were sold. We can match those dates with when Merrill was released from prison. It may not be accurate but it just might narrow the search. What do you think?'

Tony grinned. 'Sounds just perfect. What does the boss keep saying, "Keep an open mind" and with that we may as well be creative. Thanks, Kasum.'

* * *

The taxi pulled into the Costco car park. Danny and Jimmy climbed out. Jimmy paid. As the car pulled away, they looked across at the large block that made up the collection of apartments within the converted warehouse.

'Our friend's in there, and he's probably not alone. I've been before, only the once, to remind him to look after you when you were released from the nick. He owed me big time. I never went again. I was asked but I don't like him nor his arrogant ways. All our other communication was by phone.'

Danny looked at his father. 'You really cared about me didn't you, even though you knocked me from pillar to post?'

Turning, Jimmy put a hand on his shoulder and nodded, it was subtle but it was there. 'Care? All I know is that's how I was brought up, it wasn't an easy childhood, and that's what I learned about parenting. There's no handbook given when you become a parent, but let me tell you one thing, I was kinder and more generous than my old man was to me, that's for sure. Your Mum's dad was a right bastard too, bloody strict and hard, probably worse than mine. Gave me a couple of good hidings after we were married when she ran home in tears and the drink had got the better of me. The beatings were when he was with his mates and never when I was sober. Things might well have been different if he'd tried when he was on his own.' He started walking towards the road. 'Top gate. They have security at the gate and a load of cameras. Always enter through the front, never look for a tradesman's entrance. The more confident you are, the less likely you are to be stopped. Remember, they are often comfortable in their box, often bored and probably looking at something entertaining on their phones. If we're stopped, we tell them the name of the person we're visiting and the apartment number. I know where their entrance is as the building has many and I know the process and that always helps. Remember also, Danny, we never try to exit the way we came in;

that will give us a bit of a trek but it's better to leave as few clues as possible to the fact we've paid a visit, particularly if our boys and girls in blue have solved the clues we've left them. I thought they all had to have bloody degrees these days and the clues are not really Mastermind level, so here's hoping!'

Much of the land to the north of the warehouse was in various stages of construction, and more work was taking place closer to the river.

The main road was not busy, as most of the traffic leaving Liverpool used the higher dual carriageway. They crossed using the pelican. Just as Jimmy had said, walking through the gates whilst chatting and ignoring the gatehouse worked perfectly. They listened for an order to stop but none came and they continued with the charade as they walked the length of the building. The five floors of rich red brickwork and cheese-coloured stone around the lower entrance areas impressed Danny. Workmen were power-washing grime from the lower stone and the contrast was clearly visible. There was a strength and purpose to the building and, even though it was a ware-house, to him it was as impressive as a palace.

'I've seen these all my life and never really looked at them, they're bloody beautiful!'

'Wait until you see what they've done inside, and these are nowhere near as luxurious as those in the developing Tobacco Warehouse.'

'One day, if my ship comes in, I'll have one like this, Dad. I promise.' There was a yearning sincerity in his voice and it was the first time he had used the word 'dad' without thinking. It made Jimmy pause.

'Maybe when your canal boat leaves, you'll be able to buy one, son.' He patted Danny on the back and they continued. 'Let's hope all goes to plan.'

* * *

As Mrs Beales walked down the drive, she noticed only one curtain was drawn across the living room window. She knew it had been closed to keep the late afternoon sun out of the room and off the television screen. She therefore knew where he would be and she was right in her assumption. Wayne was horizontal on the settee when she entered. The television was loud. He heard the door but did not move, only raised his voice.

'Come home, have we? Your tail between your legs as usual?' The shout came but there was little anger. 'I'd like to escape to the fucking country as well if I had any money, like these folk on here, away from the crap we have to put up with and the boredom of work. Christ, I bloody hate work, me.'

She always knew what he would be watching, he was like clockwork.

'Do you want a brew?'

She moved to the kitchen. There was a smell of fried bacon, the sink was half full of dirty dishes and a frying pan; he had obviously had a change of heart about eating. Apart from his opening gambit, he seemed calm and back in his old ways as he entered the kitchen. He said nothing for a few minutes.

'You've had enough time to think of a story as to why the coppers needed to chat with you in private. Go on, give us your best shot whilst you're making the brew. Women can do that stuff, multitask.' He pulled a chair out from the table and sat on it the wrong way round, straddling the backrest.

'Have you had a shower yet?'

Wayne shook his head. 'What for? I'm going to work not to a bloody dance. By the way, I'm all ears.'

Turning, she leaned her back against the sink, folding her arms to create a symbolic barrier between them. 'They wanted to know about my relationship with Danny.'

Wayne frowned. 'You're his neighbour, or at least you are when he's here. You could also say you're his friend, as am I. But they know that already, we told them that when they came here.'

She nodded and then he noticed her shake her head. 'That's only partly true. They wanted to know more.'

'Spill the beans woman and stop pissing me about, *Tipping Point* starts soon and you know I don't like missing it.'

'You've already done that, spilled beans.' She pointed to the cooker where the residue of his cooking was still in evidence. 'Why can't you just clean up after yourself?'

He moved quickly from the chair, as his hand raised.

'You'll do that only once, Wayne Beales, and then you'll be wallowing in your own shite for the rest of time as I won't be here to clean up after you. You might find this laughable but other men find me attractive. You can't see beyond the edge of your own world of self-pity and nastiness. Where do you go to in that head of yours?' Her confidence growing, she let her eyes settle on his. 'Or is it, Wayne Beales, you've just lost your ability to care?'

He stopped, lowering himself back onto the chair. 'You'd never understand, no one would, they can't unless ... Other men?' He laughed. 'You're kidding yourself, woman.'

'Really? The police wanted to know how long my affair with Danny Maynard had been going on.' She paused, uncertain as to Wayne's reaction as the look of incredulity unfolding across his face could not be readily interpreted. She stiffened for whatever might come her way.

* * *

There was a number of entrances to the warehouse apartments. They knew the correct one, positioned within the city-side gable. The glass doors were directly in front and the board containing the apartment numbers was to the right. Jimmy scanned them.

'You do the honours, son. That one.'

Danny let his finger rest momentarily on the stainless-steel button. A red light flickered, demonstrating it was ringing somewhere in the building. The intercom crackled and Jimmy stood in front of the camera.

'It's Jimmy. I've someone with me you've been looking for, but then you could never find your arse even with your hand in your back pocket, could you, Matthew. Or do you now prefer the name Richard?'

There was no answer but the door clicked open. Jimmy pulled a face. 'Tell it like it is and never let the cocky twat get peas above sticks. I think I might have upset him, but you just watch your old dad and learn. We will pass this way but once.'

The interior of the communal area was even more impressive than Danny had expected. The blend of the old with the modern seemed to work perfectly. The apartment door was open and Jimmy entered first, holding up a hand, indicating that Danny should wait until called.

Matthew Merrill was sitting by the window in what looked like a woven hanging chair. Briggs was standing by the metal stairs that led to the mezzanine floor.

'We've brought you this, Matthew.' He held up the pipe. 'It contains most, but not all of your goods, as the lad had expenses to pay trying to evade you and your children. It's not a lot in the grand scheme of things because he was brought up to be fair. You might put it down as an industrial injury fee.'

'Please, Matthew no longer exists, I am only known as Richard.'

'Dick to your friends? That fits you perfectly.'

The chair stopped swinging and Jimmy saw Briggs move. 'Tell that gorilla of yours to stay put as you only have my word

188

that there's anything in here.' He tapped the pipe. 'It could just be anywhere between where the taxi dropped us and here.'

Richard held up a hand towards Briggs. 'Sorry, we got off on the wrong foot, let's start again. May I offer you refreshments?'

Jimmy smiled. 'Danny!'

Danny entered.

'Richard here wants to know if you'd like a coffee or tea. I'm having tea. We'll all have tea, all of us.' He looked at Briggs emphasising the words, 'You too.'

Briggs frowned and looked at Richard for confirmation.

He nodded. 'Four teas.'

Briggs reluctantly moved into the kitchen area.

'So, in your opinion, what's fair as far as his expenses and compensation goes? Do sit,' Richard muttered allowing his seat to swing gently again.

'So, as I said, industrial injuries.' He pointed to the damage to Danny's head. 'No more than ten to fifteen grand but I know it's not that much considering what's in here.' He opened the top of the pipe and removed a plastic covered wad of notes. 'Whatever's missing from this one and that's it; the rest is untouched. The deal of the day for you is that you get all of this and Danny here, goes off your radar, he becomes free as a bird. That's the only offer.'

Richard raised his eyebrows and pulled a face as Briggs returned with four mugs on a tray, placing them on the table. He picked one up and offered it to Jimmy.

'Thanks, you're too kind, but if it's all the same to you, I'll get my own when I'm ready.' Holding the pipe across his lap he leaned forward and began shuffling the identical mugs. 'Have you ever played *Find the Lady* before, gentlemen?' He paused, taking a mug and handing it to Briggs then another to Richard. 'You two drink first.'

Briggs looked at Richard and shook his head.

'Not thirsty any longer? Funny that. Neither am I.' He opened the other end of the tube, removing a gun which he handed to Danny. Flipping off the protective paper, he immediately checked it and clicked off the safety. That gun was once yours. Remember? Now gentlemen, drink your tea and when you've drunk those, there's two more mugs here just in case lady luck is on your side.'

'You haven't got the balls, if you're anything like Danny there.'

Jimmy pushed a false smile across his face before slipping the pipe onto Danny's lap. Standing, he went in the direction of the kitchen, removed two knives from the block next to the sink and returned. He pointed to Briggs signalling him to put down his mug and place his right hand on the low table. As soon as it was flat, the blade from the larger of the two blades came down with such force it pinned his hand to the wooden top. The big man sank to his knees and cried out.

'Funny how you can't hear people scream in these old buildings. As you realise, I do have the balls ... Dick. You also have about six more knives in your knife block should I need them. Now drink your tea.' Jimmy picked up the mug Briggs put down and handed it to him. 'Ambidexterity is a skill you'll have to learn, a big word for a big man.'

Within five minutes, they had drunk the four mugs of tea.

'Now, we wait. If I'm correct, two of those contained a Mickey, or the term you'll know, Dickie, is roofie. The good old date rape drug. Do you need to use them when hunting women, Richard, or is it only for the ugly monster here to allow him to get his end away?'

CHAPTER 25

'Y ou and Danny? Sex? You're too old ... aren't you?'
'It only stopped when he went inside. Started when he was eighteen. It was my birthday gift to him. When he came out of prison, it became more frequent.'

Wayne did not respond. He was still trying to comprehend what he was hearing.

'I thought you knew or at least suspected, after all, we've not ...'

Leaning over the backrest of the chair, Wayne burst into tears. Deep and sincere sobs of pure grief erupted. 'How could you?'

She unfolded her arms, wanting to approach him but uncertain of his response. She had never seen him like this, he rarely showed any degree of emotion but she also knew he could be unpredictable. 'I'm not sorry, Wayne, if that's what you're waiting to hear. You just treated me as if I were your mother. Just look at this sink. Leave it, she'll come in and clear up. You stopped wanting me, loving me and so I sought loving elsewhere. I don't think we've been in love for years, it's only convenience and laziness. And now, you can't even be bothered to shower!'

The sobbing continued until he finally looked up. She could see the tracks of real tears running down his cheeks, his eyes were red. 'Loving?' He wiped his nose on the back of his hand. 'That with Danny wasn't loving, that was probably lust, animal lust. Maybe in the eyes of the law you were taking advantage of a child. You knew his background and all he wanted was maternal love.' He made it sound dirty and abusive.

'It wasn't like that at all,' she protested crushing her arms closer to her chest.

'It's only when you've been abused, really abused, that you understand the true harm that is done. You may never know the psychological damage he might now suffer, it could be invisible. It will run deep where he doesn't understand it, but, one day, it will surface and he may not be able to handle it. Do you not see the potential harm you've caused the lad? You should be disgusted with yourself. I feel disgusted as well as betrayed.'

'What are you trying to tell me, Wayne? Who's abused you, a neighbour, a teacher or just yourself in that head of yours?' She moved a finger to her temple.

Standing, he kicked the chair towards her. 'You disgust me with your animal acts and your lack of understanding.' Turning, he left the room.

* * *

Briggs moved his left hand.

'If you move your other hand anywhere near that knife handle, I'll pin you to this wonderful wooden floor by your balls and it would be such a shame to spoil it.' He waved the other blade. Jimmy never flinched as the threat was issued, leaving Briggs in no doubt that the threat was real and the outcome would be painful. Danny saw Jimmy's eyes and recognised an evil he had seen before. And cold fear went down his spine. Briggs moved his hand behind his back.

Richard shook his head as if trying to clear it.

'If it's what I think it might be, you'll be away to the fairies in five minutes. You're probably feeling a bit sick, maybe dizzy, feeling hot, or do you feel cold, Dickie?' Jimmy sat back watching both men in turn.

'I … I think I'm fine, you're too sus … picadus … fuck! Shit! Bast …'

Jimmy looked at Danny. 'Tried to slip us a rather large dose of Rohypnol or something similar. In a short time, they'll be out of it. If you fancy the big man, then he's all yours. I know one thing, neither will be dancing in a short while.'

'If it's okay with you, I'd rather insert wasps up my bottom.' Danny giggled whilst pulling a face. 'How did you know?'

'I didn't, just a guess. I wouldn't have offered drinks unless … It's saved us using these.' He pointed to his gun.

'Watch them, particularly Briggs, as he has a bigger frame and it might not affect him to the same extent. Dickie there might have taken both doses and therefore Briggs could be faking. If he goes for the knife or if he looks as though he could be trouble, shoot him in the groin but don't kill him, or at least not yet. They have something that belongs to us and I need to find it.'

Jimmy stood, but instead of moving away, he raised the gun and brought it down onto the side of Briggs' head. He immediately slumped onto the floor, nudging the table slightly as he fell. His right hand remained secured to the table where blood continued to pool in pulses.

'Better to be safe than sorry. Same goes for Dickie bird on his perch. If you have any doubts.'

Richard was now completely lost to the world. His mouth

gaped and saliva dribbled from the lower corner. Jimmy started his search in the room they were in before slowly and methodically working his way through the rest of the apartment.

In that moment of stillness, the calm after the storm, his father's calculated coldness and quick aggression reminded him of one Christmas Day when he had not arrived home ...

Mum fretted and fussed, wanting everything to be just so for us kids. We watched telly – we'd opened the couple of presents we each had been given.

'He's bloody late again. Danny, go down and tell your dad the bird will need carving in half an hour and not to be late or the dinner will be spoiled.'

Protesting I'd miss the film, off I went. Outside it wasn't like Christmas at all. It was mild, grey and drizzling. There was singing, laughter and loud noise from inside the pub a couple of houses away, the Slade song. Two blokes stood by the door having a fag. One had a poor dog on a lead, wet and miserable.

Inside it smelled of stale smoke. There he was, in the middle of the mayhem, holding forth, pint in hand, the king clown in a room full of clowns. Few women that I could see. He didn't hear my shout so I tugged his arm – he dropped his pint. He grabbed me, lifting me so high only the toes of my slippers were just touching the wet and sticky carpet. The hit he gave me left my ear ringing, but I heard another shout.

'Leave the lad alone, Jimmy, you fucking bully, it's your lad!'

Whoever said it, Dad turned at the same time as he let go of me, driving his fist into the face of the chap to his right. There was blood, broken teeth, chaos and commotion, but most of all there was evil in his face, in his eyes. And the stupid song still singing about a merry Christmas.

He didn't come and carve the turkey; we ate without him. Mum

cried as usual. He came home about two hours later; he never had a
care for others. Mum asked him to help clear the table: he spread his
arm and swiped most of the things onto the floor. Mum and sis disap-
peared upstairs as he grabbed bits of food and ate, demanding I bring
him beer. Soon he was snoring on the couch oblivious to the upset he
had caused. I hated him then.

In less than fifteen minutes Jimmy came back with the large,
tightly wrapped package. He also held a small box with no
label. He tipped the contents onto the table. The white
lozenge-shaped tablets scattered along the length, some dropping into the blood, the white contrasting starkly with the
deep red.

'The shits! They get a posh place, a bit of money, and they
think they're somebody special. I was right, it's Rohypnol, old
stuff too from all accounts, Danny, they now colour these green
with a blue core so they change the colour of the drink they're
slipped into. These, however, are what he added to the tea,
colourless and flavourless.' Holding the larger package, he
checked it over. 'Well, Danny Boy, they've not even opened it
yet.'

Danny immediately thought of Trevor on hearing the name,
Danny Boy.

'That's good for us. Take the cash and put it back into the
pipe. It's time to leave these two, but first ...' From his pocket he
removed some packets and some plastic ties. He secured
Richard's hands to the chain on which the chair hung from the
ceiling, before removing the knife and dragging Briggs to the
metal stairs. He repeated the same process. He searched for both
their phones and slipped them onto the table. Collecting the
packets and the firearms, he moved to the kitchen, slid open a
drawer and concealed one of the packets he had brought within.

He did the same in the bedroom and bathroom, hiding the guns too. 'It's time we left, son.'

As originally planned, they did not leave the way they had entered the site. They moved down the dockside of the property, pausing briefly to negotiate some fencing. Danny held the pipe on his shoulder whilst Jimmy tucked the package under his arm. Within five minutes, they were on Waterloo Road facing the Kingsway Tunnel ventilation shaft, an interesting building in its own right.

'We can walk from here, keeping away from the Pierhead.'

CHAPTER 26

She watched as Wayne drove his car off the drive. For somebody who had seemed so angry moments before, he drove as if nothing had happened. There was no aggression or wheel spin. Checking her watch, she realised he was much too early for work. *He'll be back when he's thought it all through and come to terms with it*, she thought as she moved back into the kitchen. She started to clear away his mess. Her mind drifted to Danny and a smile touched to her lips. She could just do with a bit of TLC right now.

Wayne was anything but calm. He was parked behind the holiday camp on the promenade at Ainsdale. He needed air, fresh air, and lots of it to clear his confusion. He did not leave the car, he just stared out of the window and stared at the sand dunes, the dune-grass waving in the stiff onshore breeze. The only people there seemed to be dog walkers and runners. Within fifteen minutes, he knew what he needed to do. He had to face the fact that things would never be the same again.

On arriving home, he went through to the kitchen; it was empty and tidy. She was in the lounge; he could hear the television. The shed was unlocked. He moved the paint tubs and pulled out a plastic container. He paused, making sure in his own mind he was doing the right thing, the right thing for him. It was about him, nobody else mattered, as they had never understood. He took out most of the contents and stashed them in one of the old paint tins but kept the item he needed. He paused and thought again. Did he really want to leave her, to start afresh? He had not been alone for so long. He watched a spider spinning a web within the net curtain. It was alone, fending for itself, so why couldn't he?

* * *

Kasum and Tony pulled up within the gates of the warehouse apartments and stopped at the barrier. Nothing seemed to happen for a few minutes, until the security officer ambled out. Kasum held up her ID and also a photograph of Richard Foley.

'Merseyside Police. We're looking for this man. Richard Foley or maybe Matthew Merrill. We believe he might he renting here.'

'A minute, I'll need my readers.' He went back into the gatehouse. 'Foley? Yes, not seen him for a couple of days. He's usually with a couple of friends when I see him, one's a big chap. He has that red car down the bottom.' His scouse accent was thick. He pointed down to the city area of the apartments. 'His entry door's on the end of the building. It's the only one.'

He went back inside and returned giving them the apartment number. 'Thought I'd just check I was correct, like. I was. Give us a moment and I'll lift the barrier.'

Within minutes, Tony was resting a finger on the button whilst chewing part of the nail on his left thumb. Once successful, he spit it out. Kasum turned away. The red light flashed, indicating they could be heard.

'Back in a mo.' Tony ran towards the security gatehouse.

'I need you now down there with a key for the apartment. It might be a matter of life or death.' He emphasised the word *death*. 'Now!' Tony tapped his desk.

After much fumbling he followed Tony. 'I'll need to be with you, you just can't go in on your own.' His breathlessness was soon apparent.

After some protestation, the security officer got his way as he would not open the apartment, unless he was to enter first. It was more than his job was worth if he let even the police in without checking with the occupant. He knocked for a second time but there was no answer.

Kasum could see Tony's face turning red with anger. 'Please open it now. We've wasted vital minutes when we could have been inside.' The electronic pass key turned to illuminate the lock green and Tony pushed the security officer out of the way and entered.

'Fuck!' Both men looked dead. 'Stay outside!' The tone of the order left neither the officer nor Kasum in any doubt as to what they should do. He moved towards Richard and checked for a pulse. 'He's alive.' He crossed to Briggs. 'He is too but his pulse is shallow and irregular. Call it in. Backup, ambulance and CSI, as soon as.' He then pointed to the security officer who was propped against the wall looking decidedly grey. 'I want CCTV footage of this block for the last thirty-six hours and I'll want to work backwards from today. Are you listening?'

Kasum nudged him. 'Did you hear and understand that?'

The man nodded.

'He'll want it in the half hour so you'll need to get clearance and have it ready. You'll also need to be prepared to let the emergency services down to here as well as the CSI, but no one else. Have you got that?'

He nodded again. It was as if he'd lost his tongue.

Tony scanned the room, the tablets, the blood, the two knives. It appeared that whoever had been there had deliberately left things for them to find, the main one being Foley.

* * *

Jimmy slipped the key into the padlock, opened the gate and they descended onto the jetty before making their way to the boat. There was a warmth to the inside of the boat after a day of sitting with the sun on the cabin roof.

'It's always good to be home.' Dumping the parcel on the seat, he put the kettle onto the gas ring. 'A proper brew is what we need. Empty the pipe here and then put it on the front of the boat. We'll get rid of it later.'

'What did you hide and why leave the guns?'

Jimmy laughed. 'Class A drugs, Danny. I popped a few grands worth around the apartment. The guns will really get them into serious trouble, particularly if they can be identified as having been used in previous crimes. A murder would be perfect for our friend, Dick. He'll be up to his neck in shit.'

'We left our fingerprints and DNA all over the place.'

He smiled again as the whistle on the kettle began to protest. 'You've led them there with your clues, our clues. They would expect to find yours. Mine? That will be a surprise to them. They've achieved what they set out to do. They'll still want you and me, but we'll be away on the boat that's just full of surprises. The pilot will come on board early tomorrow and we'll be on the Manchester Ship Canal and then the Shropshire Union before lunch. From there, it's up to us. The one thing they'll not be looking for is a canal boat. Remember, Daniel Forsythe, we're just simply enjoying the freedom of the canals. Now, take the pipe and then we'll have that brew.'

* * *

DCI Mason pulled his car into the car park and flashed his ID. Richard Foley and Briggs had been attended to by the first responder and Richard had been detained in an isolated part of the building close to his apartment. Briggs, on the other hand, had been taken to hospital. The knife damage to the hand had severed tendons and damaged bones and would require surgery. The red Volvo had been secured ready for removal and CSIs were scouring the apartment. Both firearms had been located along with the drugs. The two phones retrieved had also been sent for investigation.

Kasum stood and talked with the paramedic.

'We've identified the tablets and, depending on the quantity consumed, I believe he'll be woozy, hung over and confused for some time. He'll have difficulty moving his limbs. He may well also suffer from anterograde amnesia.'

Kasum frowned.

'Sorry, he'll not recall much, if anything at all, from when the drug took hold, even the time running up to taking it might prove to be confusing. Interviewing and receiving accurate and indeed detailed information will prove difficult and certainly unreliable. That's why they use it as a date rape drug as women and men cannot identify the perpetrator or be sure of what's happened to them. The fact that they were unconscious when you found them, particularly the big chap, tells me they'd consumed a large dose.'

Tony was tracking the CCTV in reverse time. There were eight screens, all synchronised and it was not long before the video of Danny and another adult male could be seen entering the site through the main gate. He paused it.

'Did you stop these two?' He checked the time.

The security officer dropped his glasses. 'Nope, didn't see them come in.'

'Even though they would be on these screens and had also walked past these windows here?'

'Might have been having a toilet break. We're allowed, as you might not have noticed that this isn't a high security prison, it's a collection of luxury apartments. We're here to help and to keep vehicles from parking illegally.'

Tony continued the video. He noticed the two men had kept their heads down as they progressed along the edge of the building as if they were aware of the camera positions. 'What the hell is he carrying?' He paused it again. 'Can we zoom in on that?'

'Looks like a length of pipe, soil pipe, maybe, the wide one. Black plastic possibly.'

Tony put his face closer. He was probably correct.

'It's got end caps from what I can see.' The security officer pointed to one end that was clearly visible. 'It's holding something.'

'I wonder what's in it?' Tony muttered, his curiosity now spiked.

'A shotgun maybe?'

That was always a possibility but Tony thought an unlikely one owing to the diameter of the cylinder. It was certainly long enough.

'There were no shots fired at about this time?' He read out the time shown on the lower edge of the footage.

'No, not that I remember.'

Tony was neither confident the officer would know, nor whether he would admit it as he had allowed two strangers to enter. The consequences for him were all too obvious.

Within the hour, the footage was sent to Rose Hill, to digital forensics, for a more detailed inspection and to run retrospective facial recognition. It was definitely Danny Maynard but they were uncertain as to the other man's identity.

Mason hovered at the entrance to the apartment. Fingerprints had been taken from the entrance door. Officers were interviewing occupants whose apartments overlooked the route the men had taken. There were few in occupancy at that time of day.

'Legged it over the fence, but they appeared to be taking more with them than they had when they arrived. Some kind of box or package. I assume it will be drugs, by the ease with which it was carried.'

Kasum appeared. 'He's still out of it and the paramedic thinks he will be for some time to come so he's an unreliable witness and can't be interviewed until he's fully recovered—'

'I believe you interpreted the first photograph and the one that brought us here, the end of the "odyssey" I believe you called it. You must have one of those abstract minds, Kasum. Well done,' Mason commented.

'We believe this is the result Danny wanted. We've removed a thorn from his side but to be honest, sir, we've not finished. The question is why? What's he up to? Is he taking over this pitch? Finding firearms and Class A drugs will see Merrill away, and others who might be linked to the phones we found for quite some time.'

'The evidence will direct us, and that takes time. It always does. The killer's still free and it might appear that we're no closer to finding him, but like the tides, it can change with what we've discovered, especially when we've analysed the forensics finds. Those investigating haven't gone away. We must concentrate on closing this, finding Maynard. We have the house searches planned for early tomorrow.'

The look on Kasum's face emphasised her personal involvement in the deaths of the dropouts. 'It seems to have gone so quiet since the attack on the young woman. I've researched similar past cases. They can come in spurts and then nothing before springing up again, some time in the future and often in a different location. I feel so helpless and inefficient at times, sir.'

Mason rested his hand on her shoulder. 'We'll find whoever is responsible. You have my word on that.'

CHAPTER 27

D anny stared across the water of Salthouse Dock towards the buildings that surrounded the Albert Dock. The blanket was wrapped around his legs to keep the damp evening chill out, a mug of coffee to his side. The Ferris wheel dressed in multicoloured lights contrasted starkly with the darkening river sky. To him, the scene before him encapsulated a life for which he had longed. There was a freedom and a joy, confirmed by the laughter that spilled over the water. He removed the final cigarette from the packet and read the neat writing printed down the length. The last words seemed quite prophetic, 'Time will heal! Well done, son.' Removing the lighter, he slipped the cigarette between his lips and lit it. He inhaled deeply, the tobacco stung his throat a little but he felt his shoulders relax. He pondered how long it would take before Merrill and Briggs would be found, not that he cared either way. They could die for all he cared. The sound of a siren shattered the momentary illusion as a police car sped along Strand Street above, and some distance behind, the many pontoons that protruded like stubby fingers from the dockside. *Maybe that was the cavalry racing to their aid.* His thought brought a laugh swiftly followed by a tobacco induced cough.

The boat rocked slightly as Jimmy stepped off the pontoon and on to the boat, carrying a flat pizza box.

'Shove over, I've brought food. There's a pizza bus just by the dock. I got a half and half. Ham and pineapple and a spicy job.'

Danny moved up, giving him space and half of the blanket. He inhaled the last drag before flicking the remnants of the cigarette into the water. 'We should be having fish and chips. I can't remember the last time I ate fish and chips outside like this. Lashings of vinegar and salt and the smell of the sea.'

'Blackpool, when you were a kid. It was pissing down.'

'I remember the bloody gulls tried to steal them,' Danny chuckled. 'I remember now, it rained most of the week, spent more time under the pier making sand cast ...' He did not finish the sentence.

'Tomorrow is the start of a new chapter, Danny. A clean page for both of us. We rise from the ashes of our old lives and soar onto a new page, a fresh beginning and one helped by what we now have in the boat.' He collected a piece of pizza. 'A quiet existence – how I long to live without the constant threat, the looking behind whilst at the same time, trying to look forward. A man can only do that for so long. Trust me, Danny, this is your chance to leave the past behind.'

Danny took another slice of pizza. 'This is good.'

* * *

Wayne Beales turned onto Jesse Hartley Way and parked before the temporary metal barriers closing the new road from traffic and pedestrians while further construction work in the area was taking place. In the not-too-distant future, a whole new village would be created there, bringing urban life to the once industrial area. Pausing at the surrounding boards, he admired the artist's impressions illustrating the planned development. From what was happening to other areas of the riverside it would be beautiful, people-friendly and expensive.

I'd escape to here, not the country, if I could. This is my home; this is where my heart is. His thoughts brought the same tearful emotion he had felt at home and he rested a hand on the hoarding, trying to regain his equilibrium. What he needed now was peace, a place to put his recent experiences into perspective. After all, it was Liverpool, the city of his birth, but it was also the place where his life had changed on that one fateful night, the place where he had decided he should die.

Rounding the barrier that was positioned above the canal, he balanced and squeezed, managing to negotiate the metal obstruction, barriers that were only there when the building workers stopped for the day. The new road leading to the partially constructed roundabout was empty. Looking at the circle, he thought it would be a wonderful location for a statue of Jesse Hartley, the first full-time dock engineer in the world and the man responsible for the very ground on which he stood. In his mind's eye he could see it, a man from the past, cast in bronze and, in death, larger than life itself. Maybe he would be looking towards the city, a location made wealthy and diverse by the very docks he designed and built.

Wayne had one more obstacle to negotiate, another balancing act on the edge of the dock, a moment confronting an overhang above the darkening water of the Mersey. The new paving had been laid to that point, beyond which was still a derelict wasteland containing the ruined and the old. He had his target in sight. As the lowering light spread myriad colours in the western sky, he trudged past the stone building, a miniature castle that once controlled the river locks. He passed two corroding iron bridges that were more a filigree of rust than strong steel and onto what appeared to be an island, a lonely place separated from its surroundings apart from the umbilical footbridge to either edge. It was dominated by the clock tower, a giant chess piece comprising six sides. For it, and now for him, time stood still.

Plonking himself within the doorway, he stared across the Mersey and the ever-growing number of lights from across the water on the Wirral. They contrasted with the river's murkiness that ran with the tide just below him before gradually disappearing into darkness. Ignoring the chill of the wind, he removed an envelope from his jacket pocket. With what light remained, he scrolled through the cuttings. Many were printed from the internet, detailing the deaths of the homeless and the police requests for help. Further down, as if wrapped in a protective layer by the new, was the old, a news cutting, a real piece of newsprint, this too held the key words, 'Homeless men'. Wayne Beales, for the third time in twenty-four hours, broke down but there, in this isolated place, only the ancient walls were privy to his pain.

CHAPTER 28

The three police vans, including one holding police dog, moved and parked along the road, blocking the driveways of the houses belonging to Stanley Nellist and the Beales. There were no sirens and no blue strobes. The team had been briefed, each having clear instructions as to their part in the operation. This action was not about preserving forensic evidence but about collecting possible illegal or incriminating goods. If luck was on their side, finding Danny Maynard curled up in bed, in the shed or the garage would be a bonus. Owing to the discovery of firearms at the apartment the previous late afternoon, a team of firearms officers had been allocated and Mason had worked closely with their lead officer.

They would enter through the front doors using enforcers, or as they liked to call them, 'the big red key'. The dog first, then a sweep, if necessary detain and then be out, to be swiftly followed by the search teams. As with all firearms intervention, a doctor was on standby, but also knowing Nellist's medical condition, it was an additional benefit. Sitting in the control caravan a little further up the road, Mason checked his watch and also the screens showing the bodycam images of the attending officers. All were linked with mics and earpieces. The order to enter was given just after five, as spotlights illuminated the fronts of the properties.

Although the process of entering, the shouts, calls and orders, seemed disorganised, it was in reality a well-rehearsed procedure, an action that was swift, safe for all concerned, and efficient. Within minutes, the firearms officers attending one house were clear, it was the second house where there was a delay.

'We have a body, female, in the lounge. Dead on our arrival. The rest of the house and outbuildings are clear.'

Without delay, the doctor moved from the van. The reflective strips on his red medical rucksack shone brightly in the floodlights.

The room was lit, giving the doctor an immediate view of the body. Mrs Beales was positioned on the sofa. Her head, wrapped in a thin carrier bag, was hanging from the seat cushion. Her right arm was touching the floor, her left trapped beneath her whilst her legs seemed to be totally deformed as if she had suffered a serious spasm. A considerable amount of blood had soaked into the cushion's edge as well as the carpet directly below her head. There were other stains but they seemed old. Conscious this was now a crime scene, there would be limited entry and the doctor was careful to touch as little as possible.

The doctor removed the bag. There was no pulse to her neck. Her eyes were wide and there was a bulge to the eyeballs within the sockets. Her mouth was clamped tight and it was clear the tongue had been partially severed by her teeth.

Mason watched the images from the bodycam as the doctor worked methodically, verbalising his impressions as he did so. Mason called control requesting a search for Wayne Beales, starting at his place of work.

The doctor flicked on his headtorch. He pronounced she was dead.

The team within Nellist's house had found him asleep in the chair, the television still on despite the commotion. Apart from a few obscenities, he seemed only confused and angry at the manner in which they had entered his house. His breathing appeared fine and the doctor was not required, but one of the firearms team, a first aider, came back to monitor his condition as delayed shock could occur.

It was Tony, rummaging through the cupboards in what was Danny's room, that made him pause. It was a series of school-type exercise books. Tony had thought little of his discovery initially until he opened one and started to read.

* * *

Beales had shivered in the tower doorway until he could stand the growing cold no longer. He needed to enter the tower. A stiff shoulder charge burst the wooden door from the door jamb, causing dormant birds to flutter. Their flapping seemed too close and he flinched. Some took flight, circling the castellated top before settling again. The door had not been locked but had been secured at some point by five long screws through the door jamb that had hardly penetrated the door itself. Maybe this precaution had been to prevent the wind blowing it open, rather than to stop the curious or needy from entering. The wood was also in poor condition and it had soon surrendered to the impact.

He felt better immediately, now that the wind was no longer present. The floor, a carpet of bird droppings, emitted a strong stench but it was warmer. Switching on the torch on his phone he looked around. Graffiti, both drawn and written, was evident. He placed the container he had brought from the garage and the fold of papers on the floor beneath the short flight of steel stairs that took him to the next level. The clock mechanism, long past its best, clung to the six walls. The spiral stairs enticed him higher. Here the first light of the day was penetrating the slits within the walls. The birds flew again, this time with a greater urgency, as he emerged, but it was the final challenge, the almost perpendicular ladder that took him out onto the top of the tower. Turning through three-hundred-and-sixty-degrees, Liverpool, his city, lay before him. The light from his torch was like a beacon.

* * *

It took an hour to obtain details from ANPR, tracking Beales's car to a point within the city. The construction workers were quick to report the car partially blocking Jesse Hartley Way. Mason addressed Skeeter.

'You can do no more here. Meet April and others at this point,' he pointed to the car's location. 'We've also had a call from security at the new Everton Stadium site to say they believe there's someone at or on the Victoria Tower. It could be Beales but … from what I can see there are only two ways to get to the island containing the tower and that's either through the new Everton stadium area or via Jesse Hartley Way. It's as if the place has its own moat! I've requested an aerial and a dog team to meet you there.'

Within fifteen minutes, Skeeter pulled up alongside four other police vehicles. She immediately spotted Steve setting up the drone. The police dog remained in the van for the time being. A number of officers stood by the fencing.

'April wants the drone up first. There's a lot of foliage and a few derelict buildings so our man could be anywhere. If he's there, the thermal imaging and these cameras will find him.

There's a large screen in the van and I'll be operational in minutes. We've informed the CAA that we're flying within the Liverpool airspace. We have a transponder on the drone making it visible to them on radar.' He grinned and carried on with the set up.

Skeeter did not fully understand the technical side but leaned into the van. The officer monitoring the images watched as the drone rose into the air. Within seconds it had gained height and was approaching the tower. The glow of body heat on the upper level was quickly detected. Steve paused the drone. Flying closer he flicked on the high-powered spotlight concentrating on the area.

'Male, just going back into the building.' Officers had already begun to move along the same route Beales had. The dog was wearing protective boots as he was brought from the van. The state of the ground was hazardous, littered with sharp metal fragments and glass. The handler followed the group but would remain as backup.

'He's out of the door. He's standing close to the edge overlooking the river.'

The commentary could be heard by each officer as they made their way to the man-made island.

'Keep them back just in case he jumps. There's a fast tide running.'

The officers paused.

'He's sitting, his legs are over the side.'

'I'll jump. Leave me alone.' The directional mic on the drone picked up his plea.

'It's Beales, confirmation it is Wayne Beales.' April sounded tense. The last thing she wanted was for him to enter the water. 'We have a Hostage and Crisis Negotiator on the way. Nobody moves closer. Bring the drone away as far as possible but maintain visual contact.'

Steve moved the drone to mid-river and used the zoom to monitor Beales.

The Marine Rescue Unit left the Pierhead and was soon moving upriver. It would hold off at a safe distance and await further instructions.

The unmarked car pulled up by the new roundabout, blue strobes within the windscreen and grille being the only indication it was a police vehicle. DI Clare Winstanley moved to the Incident Unit van. A brief introduction followed.

'What do we have?'

'Male, he is out of the tower and on the edge of the river. It's likely he murdered his wife late last night. He's been here maybe since then.'

April checked through the images of Beales.

'How close are your officers?'

Again, they used the images from the drone. 'I'm going forward. I'll need two life vests and a blanket. I've brought a flask of hot coffee and some chocolate. He'll be cold, hungry and confused.'

Slipping on a fluorescent jacket and then the life jacket, she began to move along the dockside. She needed to be seen and heard, seen as someone who was not there to judge but to help.

CHAPTER 29

Jimmy was asleep and Danny sat at the galley table. The map detailing the route Jimmy had planned was before him. It detailed the locks and swing bridges they would face once on the Shropshire Union Canal. He liked the map and studied the place names with care.

The weather was true to the forecast, although the light misting on the water brought with it cool air and dampness. Looking through the round portal, he watched as two swans approached with a glide before turning away, almost vanishing in the mist. He checked the time. The pilot was due in less than an hour. He woke Jimmy.

* * *

Clare Winstanley crossed the second metal bridge but waited once she had her feet on the island. She needed a safe distance between them, not for her safety but his.

Wayne had watched her steady approach but had not responded.

'My name's Clare, Wayne. I'm here to help. I'll not come any closer unless you want me to. I've brought some coffee, chocolate, a blanket, and this. She held up the life vest. I'm going to leave them here and go back over that second bridge. You must be cold and thirsty. When you have them and you are where you want to be, may I come back to talk with you?'

She placed the items on the ground and moved away. Wayne remained seated but he watched. He also observed the drone, it's strobe lights still bright in the dawn sky, as well as the rescue boat. Within minutes of her arriving at the second bridge, he stood, stretched and collected the items. He took the chocolate, flask and the blanket but left the life vest.

Once he was settled, Clare moved back. When she spoke, she was neither compromising nor threatening. Wayne sat huddled in the blanket drinking coffee; the chocolate had quickly been eaten. She knew from experience that there was no set time to resolve these interventions. It would take as long as it took. She changed tack, talking about Liverpool and the docks and, in particular, the island on which he sat but she received little in reply.

On finishing the coffee, he tossed the cup over the edge and watched its fall until it hit the water. He then stood and turned to Clare.

'I've carried the burden long enough, no one, not even you could possibly understand, but I shouldn't have done what I've done. I shouldn't have killed them. I just couldn't stop myself. Each one owed me a life I had lost ... I'm sorry, truly. This is not the way I wanted things to end but ... It's been like a cancer that's eaten me away, changed me from the person I was to this, the pathetic devil I am now.' He paused looking first over the edge and then back at Clare. 'I loved her, you know, I truly did. That's hard for you to believe as you know what I've done, but I did. Despite her infidel ...' He started to cry. Turning, he looked towards the tower.

Clare instinctively believed he was preparing to fall backwards rather than jump; many suicides turned away from the drop before falling, maybe it was easier.

'It's time. I'm sorry, I'm truly sorry!'

She watched as he moved back into the tower. Within a few minutes he appeared on the upper floor and mounted the castellated wall. Spreading his arms, he balanced allowing his body to stiffen as if suddenly becoming petrified and rigid. Without another word he leapt forward, trying to breach the distance between the tower's upper lip and the edge of the dock. To Clare, the leap and then the arcing fall seemed to be in silent slow motion. His body twisted in the air as if stretching to make the distance before crashing onto the stone edge. The thud was both loud and sickening and she instinctively turned away.

The drone moved in, locking on to the falling figure. The rescue boat came too, leaving a large curving wake of white foam. Wayne's unconscious body teetered on the edge before slipping into the river some distance below. Clare moved quickly to the bloodied edge and looked down into the swirling water. From the rush of the current against the dock wall, she could see the tidal flow was strong. She waited, watching the spot where Wayne had entered but there was nothing other than myriad bubbles breaking the surface. She knew that if he were still breathing on hitting the water, the lungs would quickly fill and he might not immediately come to the surface.

The rescue boat allowed the current to carry it in the hope the body would appear. She waited and watched. Skeeter moved over the bridge.

'You did all you could. There was no way he was not going in.'

Entering the tower, Skeeter moved up the stairs; enough light now penetrated for her to see. Emerging at the top she saw the hypodermic. It was clean. The small container holding a pad of what looked like tissue had also been discarded. The wad of paper, his collection of cuttings, fluttered in the light breeze. There was no need for forensic investigation, not now, not after what she had just witnessed. Collecting the items, she returned to the lower level. A number of officers were now present. As she crossed the bridge, the sun broke over the hill and a warmth purged the cold and the early dawn. The sound of the drone some distance away could still be heard.

* * *

Tony sat at his desk with the notebooks he had found in Danny's room. Kasum was at her desk.

'These are bloody heartbreaking. You shouldn't feel sorry for people like Maynard but when you understand what he had to put up with from his father, and then the blokes his mother knocked about with, you can't help but feel a certain sympathy. How anyone could be normal after all that is beyond me. There doesn't seem to have been a day when he wasn't physically abused for something.' He flicked through the pages. 'Fist, belt, rolling pin, hammer. The weapon of punishment is highlighted at the bottom of each page. Two on some occasions!'

Kasum approached and picked one up. 'I see he was running drugs for the boyfriends from ...' She looked at the date. 'He can only have been about seven, maybe eight. That was his norm. How can adults expect a child to miraculously be any different if they are brought up like this? It's not an on-and-off switch, it's a learned and expected behaviour.'

'And now?' Tony dropped the notebook and swung back in his chair whilst looking at the photographs on the whiteboard. 'He's cleared the way, got rid of the man who controlled him, Matthew Merrill, or should we say Richard?'

'Do you think he'll move up a level, fill his shoes?'

'Probably. He may still have the cash but not the guns, they were found in the flat.' There was a hint of speculation in his voice as well as doubt within the answer.

'He could have nothing and maybe that's what he wanted. Could he have just wanted those people arrested? We, and not him, get the thorn from his side so he can live a different life. The only other way he could have done that was to move away or use the firearms.'

'I'm sure time will tell when he graces our cells at some point in the future. You want a brew?'

* * *

Arcanum passed through the Brunswick Dock and waited within the lock that allowed the boat onto the Mersey. The pilot had spent time gaining permissions to move, as well as checking the boat's certification, but finally they were on their way. All three stood at the back of the boat as Liverpool slowly shrank as they moved upstream. Although the light swell on the river was calm to most river and sea craft, to a canal boat it seemed stronger, making the boat bob like a cork. Once they had crossed to travel down near the far bank the water calmed. It would not be long before they would be entering the Manchester Ship Canal, and then turning off into Ellesmere Port and the beginning of the Shropshire Union Canal.

Danny had been given permission by the pilot to move to the front of the boat now they were in calmer water. The thrum of the engine seemed hypnotically soporific. He watched a cormorant sitting on a green buoy, wings outstretched, drying in the morning sun; the river, mirror-like was almost golden and in that moment the world seemed a magical place. He had done it – against the odds he had done it!

CHAPTER 30

M ason and Decent were the last to enter the briefing. The time on the wall clock was 12.58. It had already been a busy day. Wayne Beales's body had been brought from the water twenty-seven minutes after it had entered. It would take time and a full autopsy to determine the finer details leading to his death but they were in no doubt he was dead minutes after hitting the water. Tests on the hypodermic would also take time.

Professor Joseph Lee, the forensic pathologist, had already inspected Mrs Beales's body. There was clear evidence of needle damage to the right side of her neck and further tests would determine if any drug or substance had been administered. Looking at the deformity within the limbs, his professional judgement at this early juncture suggested potassium chloride. The final piece of evidence implicating Beales as the killer of the homeless was in the documents found at the scene – the printout of the police social media requests for information for each case. It was the real news cutting on which they focused as it was displayed on the screen. Skeeter stood.

'According to this, when he was ten, he came home intoxicated, bloodied and beaten. He told his parents he had been attacked by two homeless drunks when he was exploring an empty house. Rows of terraced houses were being prepared for demolition in the area they lived. He explained that they'd beaten him and forced him to drink. What else occurred if that's the case is anyone's guess but there was never a suggestion of sexual impropriety. According to our records, the incident was reported by his parents and officers were dispatched. He was interviewed but there was no evidence of the men at the location he described. Further investigation suggested he had purchased alcohol and consumed it. The belief was that he fell heavily a number of times causing the injuries to himself. The story was believed to be a complete fabrication to hide his own misdemeanour. What appears to be strange is that he continued to protest his innocence and that he was telling the truth.'

She removed the papers selecting one: the news cutting. The image on the screen changed. On the back was written this note. It was dated, three days ago:

I never told a lie. They did what they did and much more. More than I, as a child, could speak about. Actions that damaged me more than my parents could ever realise. The police were really not interested and my parents seemed too embarrassed to fight for me. What I have done is wrong and I am sorry but I've lived too long in the shadow of the truth. Maybe people will see me through different eyes and although they still might judge they might find it in themselves to forgive. It's now the time as the tide can no longer wait!

Skeeter remained standing. 'I believe he knew about the casual sex with Danny. The way to counter that was to try to expose him to harm. He took small quantities from the goods Danny asked him to hold or where Danny stashed them in the shed; nothing too suspicious, just enough to be noticed. It worked. The day Danny came crashing through his door bleeding and frightened was the day he knew he was winning. He was a man again. What he wanted, I believe, was Danny gone, removed and possibly killed.'

Tony spoke. 'Hence the phone and the clues. He was confused as he hadn't taken anything. He hadn't creamed money nor drugs.'

'Correct.'

'So why potassium chloride?'

'He worked in the food industry. It's used in that industry as a salt replacer. He obviously knew it had other qualities and he probably learned that from talking with Stanley Nellist. That's to be confirmed, but he may well not have been complicit. We know Stanley liked to talk. The PPE we found hidden in the shed also came from his place of work. The scenario, in my opinion, didn't happen overnight, it's been a steady plan that suddenly got out of hand. Maybe he felt like a man again, powerful and in control. Who knows the workings of a person living with these mental issues.'

Kasum spoke. 'But from all accounts, Danny is not bright enough to formulate a complex set of clues to find a solution to the dilemma in which he unwittingly found himself. He must have had help.'

April answered that with information she had just received. 'The man we see him with entering the apartment complex could well be that missing link, the last jigsaw piece. We have identified him.' She paused and scanned the room. DCI Mason flicked his eyebrows as if he were party to what was about to be revealed. 'Confirmation came in from both fingerprints and DNA that it is none other than the man Danny loved to hate ... his father. It didn't take long for retrospective facial recognition to confirm that fact.'

Silence prevailed.

CHAPTER 31

The steady beat of the boat's engine ran through the vessel like a pulse. The day was warm and Danny stood holding the tiller. The passage from Ellesmere Port was busy but easy, and the countryside had opened out on either bank. After consultation they would stop in Chester to restock the boat before moving on. There was no long-term forward plan. The intention was to travel until dusk and move on at first light. According to the Boater's Guide Danny had read, there were no locks until Chester and their planned opening times had been checked. He was relatively unfamiliar with the lock system and hoped volunteer keepers would be on hand on arrival.

As with each morning, the whisky bottle had sat on the small table and had been ignored before being returned, but today was different: today was special because of their success and the fact that there had been a reconciliation. The money was now stashed in the small suitcase. Jimmy had removed the bottle top and grabbed two shot glasses pouring healthy measures. He brought them to the aft deck. The air was clean and the view over fields and trees a welcome change from the city.

Handing a drink to Danny he tapped the rim.

'It's been a long time since I touched this stuff but I know I can stop now. I don't need it to live anymore. I'm proud of you, you know that. Not everyone would have had the bottle to do what you've done. I'd watched you for some time in my journeys in and out of the city.' He tapped Danny's youthful photograph trapped behind the protective Perspex. 'When Merrill told me you were on the take, I knew there'd be trouble for you. I also knew that you wouldn't do that. When I made contact, you listened.'

Holding the glass to the light he admired the colour before bringing it to his nose. 'To *Arcanum* and to us, Danny Boy.' The contents disappeared in one.

Over the next hour Danny watched the bottle slowly drain. Jimmy had burst into song, 'It's not the leaving of Liverpool ...'

Danny concentrated on the boat his glass still full.

Jimmy emerged unsteadily from the cabin, an empty bottle in one hand. 'As luck would have it I have another somewhere.' His speech slurred. 'I hope it's in that locker to the side of you.' He tilted the bottle he held, draining the final dregs before tossing it into the canal.

At this point, several canal boats were moored to the right and the towpath ran to the left. Some looked to have been left for some time. Danny could see a bridge-like gantry crossing the waterway a few hundred yards ahead. It immediately reminded him of one of the photographs he had left in the camera. It appeared to be of a large pipe. Jimmy leaned into the cubby hole and started to pull items out discarding them on the deck.

'Where the fuck is it?'

Danny snapped the tiller in his direction. Already unstable, Jimmy turned trying to grab anything to gain stability but his efforts were in vain. Passing beneath the gantry he overbalanced slipping over the side into the middle of the canal. Danny quickly glanced behind as his father went under. Slowing the boat to almost a standstill he watched the man fight to stay afloat. Surprisingly, he was silent possibly more out of panic. When he did open his mouth, he swallowed water. Before he vanished beneath the mud brown surface, Danny could hear him spluttering and choking.

Stopping the boat, he let it drift momentarily before putting the engine in reverse. As he did so, a cyclist rode past. Ironically it was red, the same as the one on the front of the boat. The rider waved and continued unaware of what had just occurred.

Looking down, Jimmy could see his father's motionless body, his arms spread and his feet and legs lower in the water and almost invisible. There was no movement. With a boat hook he pushed the body deeper and towards the far bank trying to trap it between and under two dilapidated boats. He paused when he read the worn and weathered name painted to the flank of the smaller of the two – *Ghost*.

Within minutes, the body was no longer visible. *Arcanum* had one more secret to hold and Danny had a new notebook to fill.

* * *

The mid-morning light brought many shadows to the Parish Church gardens as Kasum walked past the church doors. She turned briefly and looked across, first at the bell and then at the statue of the homeless Jesus. By the feet was the bouquet of flowers she had reverently placed. She had spent some moments thinking of each of the victims, people who had chosen a different path in life but had seen that path cut short.

The bronze was cold to the touch as she arranged the flowers and read the note she had written:

To the many lonely people resting within this wonderful city, my heart goes out to you.

CHAPTER 32

Six Days later

April stood on the beach; Tico seemed to watch a gull's flight with interest. The autopsy had confirmed Wayne Beales had not injected himself, but toxicology showed Mrs Beales had died from a massive poisoning by potassium. It was as they had surmised. There was still a continuing search for the Maynards, but they had nothing from CCTV after the event. Requests put out on the police socials had also brought nothing, other than the usual nuisance calls.

* * *

The office was quiet, she could hear Skeeter and Tony laughing down the corridor. The usual epistle was attached to the computer screen.

Good morning, April, I think I've had a breakthrough whilst enjoying my lunch tonight. A swift follow-up has been requested with colleagues in Cheshire. The final photograph sent to you by Maynard is, I believe, a photograph of a piece of willow pattern. It was the shade of blue and the blurred edging with the white glaze that got me thinking in the weird way I often do. I've attached a photograph of a standard pattern. You will see this is English Willow Pattern. Strangely, and I think of little relevance, Liverpool used to be a manufacturing centre.

The piece in the photograph is part of the boat. Understanding the story is of escape, from land to sea to land, I contacted the Port Authority. I had little luck regarding crew listings for ships leaving Liverpool both commercial and cruise. However, I made enquiries with the river pilots. They had a canal boat leave Salthouse Quay six days ago with a pilot to travel down the Mersey with the intended onward route being the Shropshire Union Canal. The crew was a James and Daniel Forsythe. The boat is registered to James Forsythe and has been for quite some time. He has been travelling the same route on a number of occasions and I'll leave you to consider the reason – the slow boat – China – Willow pattern. Another inventive way to ship drugs? And the name of the boat I hear you whisper in my dreams? Arcanum *which means "Secret". How appropriate is that?*

The police will be patrolling the canal, a main cycle route. We know the boat hasn't passed through the lock system at Chester.

Good luck and good night.

Michael.

PS I'm going to be a father again! I guess you're stuck with me!

Skeeter came in with two coffees followed by Tony. She glanced at his shoes. There was now a definite sign of polish. She nodded. 'Well done!'

A broad smile came to his lips.

'Read that.' April pointed to the note.

Skeeter and Tony read it and then smiled. 'We'll get those bastards yet.' Skeeter announced as she continued reading. 'Bloody hell, where do they find the time, they're like ships that pass ...' She giggled.

'Maybe slow boats!' Tony mumbled.

They knocked the mugs together. 'To happy families.'

'To our move and to the team. Well done!' April looked at each person in turn.

Skeeter thought of Steve. He seemed to be occupying a lot of her thoughts recently. It was a good feeling.

Twenty-four hours later

Arcanum had been abandoned on an isolated stretch of the canal. It had the appearance of the *Mary Celeste*. When the officer managed to board the boat, the stove was still warm and two empty tumblers sat on the roof. There was no sign of Danny and Jimmy. It would be another two days before a body was dredged from the canal two miles from where the boat was discovered. Danny Maynard had disappeared to become another statistic, one of the many who go missing.

* * *

Helen collected the empty plates from the waterside table and her phone vibrated. She answered.

'You gave me your number, remember a while back. Do you want to know a secret?'

She giggled. 'What secret?' She turned to look around worried her manager would see her on the phone. She paused. Through the wall of glass, she spotted him standing next to the model of the *Titanic*; her own image was reflected as if two faces were now looking at her. His expression made her heart skip a beat.

THE VICTORIA TOWER
ALSO KNOWN LOCALLY AS 'THE
DOCKER'S CLOCK'

If my memory serves me correctly, I first saw this wonderful piece of Victorian architecture when I was being interviewed by Rebecca and Adrian for the Hobcast Book Show, the weekly podcast from Hobeck Books. They came up to Liverpool for a chat and to see for themselves some of the places mentioned within the series. It was a very different time as it was at the point when some businesses were just beginning to open after the pandemic.

For a writer, however, it is not just the building but its position within the docklands themselves that I find compelling and soon it will be within a ball kick of the new Everton football stadium, a venue that will be filled with emotion, song and festival – a far cry from the original concept and design by Jesse Hartley for an area that sits clearly on the edge of the land.

The tower is Grade II listed and is situated in Vauxhall. It is dated 1848, and was built by the engineer, Jesse Hartley. Its construction is granite rubble with a battered round base comprising round-arched window and entrances. The upper part is hexagonal, with a bracketed balcony. The mid-section, also six sides, holds a clock face to each along with paired slits with transoms above. Above these are positioned blind roundels. There is a date on the south side that can be seen from afar. It has a battlemented parapet on machicolations to top off the tower giving it the appearance of a huge chess piece.

The description of the three types of stairs and steps within this story is, to my knowledge, still authentic; the fireplaces are also still visible, but weather and vandalism have taken their toll.

The purpose of the tower was to give incoming and exiting shipping accurate time measurement. It also houses a bell that warned of impending meteorological changes, such as high tide and fog. Upon its completion, it also served as a flat for the pier master.

The clock is visible from the city looking up the docks and is testament to the fine craftsmanship and design of the Victorian period.

THE MERSEYSIDE CRIME SERIES

Praise for The Merseyside Crime Series

'Another must buy series.' ★★★★★

'I love words and this author is a master of painting a picture you can fall right into.' ★★★★★

'A stunning and flawless read.' ★★★★★

'OK I am hooked Mr Hollingdrake, I don't mind which book you write next but please write it soon!' ★★★★★

'Absolutely brilliant!' ★★★★★

Catch as Catch Can

Available in ebook, paperback and audiobook.

Syn

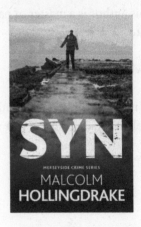

Available in ebook, paperback and audiobook.

ABOUT THE AUTHOR

You could say that the writing was clearly on the wall for anyone born in a library that they might aspire to be an author but to get to that point, Malcolm Hollingdrake has travelled a circuitous route.

Malcolm worked in education for many years, even teaching for a period in Cairo before he started writing, a challenge he longed to tackle for more years than he cares to remember.

Malcolm has written a number of successful short stories and has more than ten books available (and more to come).

Born in Bradford and spending three years in Ripon, Malcolm has never lost his love for his home county, a passion that is reflected in the settings of thirteen Harrogate Crime Series novels.

Malcolm has enjoyed many hobbies including works by Northern artists; the art auctions offer a degree of excitement when both buying and certainly when selling. It's a hobby he has bestowed on DCI Cyril Bennett, of his characters in the Harrogate Crime Series.

ACKNOWLEDGMENTS

It has been so good to meet April, Skeeter and the team again in the wonderful setting of Merseyside. It is always refreshing to wander the docks and feast on the wonderful architecture that is so easily taken for granted. Pleasing also is to see the development taking place, the creative vision breathing new life into the past so the area can enjoy a prosperous future. That creativity enhances and does not destroy, it opens our eyes to the quality and detail our ancestors felt necessary to infuse even into the most mundane of industrial buildings and structures. I believe the secrets of the tunnels, drains and pipe works beneath the docks have still to be understood fully as the original plans no longer survive.

My first thanks must go to the people of Liverpool who have answered the many questions I have asked when writing this book. A shout out to the lock keepers at the Stanley Flight who work with and volunteer to support the Canal and River Trust. They were most helpful. To Sid, of Sid's Ditch fame I doff my cap, as without the ditch boats would not be able to travel into the docks from the Leeds and Liverpool Canal. I must also say thank you to the many boatmen and women travelling the canal for putting up with my questioning.

The wonderful and hospitable staff at the Titanic Hotel. You were truly helpful, tolerant and patient. You are a credit to your profession, thank you.

To Gary Barton and Brian Price for your advice on technical matters, thank you.

To my ever-patient wife, Debbie. I can never thank you enough for casting your eye over the manuscript and giving me honest feedback. Love you. x

To Helen Gray for your professional proofing as always. Thank you.

To Ian Cleverdon for all the support and encouragement. Thank you to Bill Sass, a man who has policed Liverpool for more years than he cares to remember. An inspiring chat.

I would like to give a mention to the two Annes who found friendship through my books. Who would have thought books could have that power?

I would like to extend my thanks to the Hobeck Advanced Readers' Team for their guidance, support and dedication. You do a marvellous job.

Thanks to Dave and Jan Johnson for allowing Skeeter to take over their cottage for the period of this book. I hope she left it tidy!!

All writers need their names whispered far and wide. This never happens magically but by bloggers, readers' groups and internet groups who turn their hobby into a support system for writers and authors. By administering social media groups, interviewing and talking about books to a broader audience they bring authors into many homes. Thank you. This is true of those working in radio. Emma and Martin Truelove and Michelle Barlow, you have been wonderful.

Thank you to Katie Spencer. Her album, *The Edge of the Land*, inspired the title of this book. It is a beautiful and haunting collection of songs.

A special thank you to Helen, David White and Murphy for your support of my books.

Thanks to Calum Parodi for his contributions and his enthusiastic support.

To Hobeck Books, thank you for having confidence in my

work and for the dedication you put in to making it the best it can be.

Finally, it is to you, dear readers, to whom I must say a massive thank you for supporting my writing.

Best wishes,

Malcolm

HOBECK BOOKS – THE HOME OF GREAT STORIES

This book is the third in the Merseyside Crime Series.

If you've enjoyed this book, please visit Malcolm's website: **www.malcolmhollingdrakeauthor.co.uk** to read about his other writing, inspirations, writing life and for news about his forthcoming writing projects.

Hobeck Books offers a number of short stories and novellas, free for subscribers in the compilation *Crime Bites*.

- *Echo Rock* by Robert Daws
- *Old Dogs, Old Tricks* by AB Morgan
- *The Silence of the Rabbit* by Wendy Turbin
- *Never Mind the Baubles: An Anthology of Twisted Winter Tales* by the Hobeck Team (including many of the Hobeck authors and Hobeck's two publishers)
- *The Clarice Cliff Vase* by Linda Huber
- *Here She Lies* by Kerena Swan
- *The Macnab Principle* by R.D. Nixon
- *Fatal Beginnings* by Brian Price
- *A Defining Moment* by Lin Le Versha
- *Saviour* by Jennie Ensor
- *You Can't Trust Anyone These Days* by Maureen Myant

Also please visit the Hobeck Books website for details of our other superb authors and their books, and if you would like to get in touch, we would love to hear from you.

Hobeck Books also presents a weekly podcast, the Hobcast, where founders Adrian Hobart and Rebecca Collins discuss all things book related, key issues from each week, including the ups and downs of running a creative business. Each episode includes an interview with one of the people who make Hobeck possible: the editors, the authors, the cover designers. These are the people who help Hobeck bring great stories to life. Without them, Hobeck wouldn't exist. The Hobcast can be listened to from all the usual platforms but it can also be found on the Hobeck website: **www.hobeck.net/hobcast**.

Finally, if you enjoyed this book, please also leave a review on the site you bought it from and spread the word. Reviews are hugely important to writers and they help other readers also.

ALSO BY MALCOLM HOLLINGDRAKE

Bridging the Gulf
A thriller set in Yorkshire and Cyprus

The Harrogate Crime Series
Only the Dead
Hell's Gate
Flesh Evidence
Game Point
Dying Art
Crossed Out
The Third Breath
Treble Clef
Threadbare
Fragments
Uncertainty of Reason
The Damascene Moment
Trapped Secrets

Also by Malcolm Hollingdrake

Short Story
'A Piece of Paper that Changed a Life' published in the charity
anthology, *Everyday Kindness*, edited by L. J. Ross